# THE RED INSECTS

Nick Hansley, his wife Ena and father-in-law find that their country house, The Cedars, radiates a positively evil aura. Their strange neighbour Dr. Lexton calls, wanting to buy their home. But who is Dr. Lexton? And as for Ena's deceased uncle, entomologist Cyrus Odder, what was the nature of the secret experiment he had worked on there? Then after a mysterious death in the house — death spreads its net across the countryside — and the entire world . . .

JOHN RUSSELL FEARN

$\blacklozenge$

# THE RED INSECTS

*Complete and Unabridged*

# LINFORD
*Leicester*

First published in Great Britain

First Linford Edition
published 2010

British Library CIP Data

Fearn, John Russell, *1908 – 1960*.
   The red insects.- -(Linford mystery library)
   1. Science fiction.
   2. Large type books.
   I. Title II. Series
   823.9'12–dc22

   ISBN 978–1–44480–143–9

Published by
F. A. Thorpe (Publishing)
Anstey, Leicestershire

Set by Words & Graphics Ltd.
Anstey, Leicestershire
Printed and bound in Great Britain by
T. J. International Ltd., Padstow, Cornwall

This book is printed on acid-free paper

# 1

## Mystery at The Cedars

The big detached house came into view as the car swept over the hill from Balton village. Nick Hansley put on the brakes and switched off the ignition — then he surveyed the scene. Beside him, his wife Ena was silent, reflecting. In the back of the car her father peered into the late autumn afternoon but made no comment.

'Looks spooky,' Nick said finally. 'Still, given house prices these days, I suppose we ought to be grateful at your having inherited it.'

Ena nodded but still did not say anything. The Cedars looked rather like something out of Edgar Allan Poe — a great rambling place, utterly alone, surrounded by leaf-bare cedar and cypress trees. From this distance it was not possible to see whether the grounds were well kept or not — probably not, since Ena's uncle — on her mother's side — had been a renowned eccentric and probably had possessed no liking for gardening.

'Spooky or otherwise,' Ena's father said, from the back of the car, 'we'd better take it over. The furniture van will be here any time.'

'The Cedars,' in fact, had been bequeathed to Ena by her recently deceased uncle. From early visits she knew it was lonely — its nearest neighbour being a house on a solitary hill a mile distant — but it seemed better than a very ordinary house in a London suburb. Ena merely carried the impressions of childhood when she had occasionally visited Uncle Cyrus with her now dead mother. Now, viewing the place as a grown woman, she felt unsure.

'I don't know why,' she said at last, 'but it doesn't look at all like I had expected. When I was here, as a girl of ten, the trees were in full leaf and it was summer time. It seemed quite divine then. But at the moment . . . '

Nick gave a grin and hugged her

shoulder. 'Can't judge by appearances,' he assured her. 'Sombre though it may be it's a better bet than the cheap suburban dump we were living in. I can always get up and down to the city in half an hour in the car anyway. Let's be moving.'

He switched on the engine again and in a few minutes had reached the massive wrought-iron gateway. Climbing out of the car he took from his pocket the big key that had been given with the bequest. Unlocking the gates he swung them wide and presently was driving up the drab, lengthy vista lined with its dreary trees that ended at the front door.

There were three steps leading up to it, worn and filthy dirty. As she climbed from the car Ena allowed her gaze to rove over the big place. It had mullioned windows of the old-fashioned type; low-built eaves, and Tudor-style chimney stacks.

'I'm still doubtful,' she commented, catching Nick's eye.

'No need to be.' He was experimenting with the keys to find the right one for the front door. 'If all else fails and we get goose-pimples we can always sell the joint to a trust for use as a college, or something.'

'Yes ... Yes, I suppose we might do that.'

Ena's father, plump and late middle-aged, huddled his coat collar round his neck as the chill autumn wind struck him. He surveyed everything carefully and sniffed.

'Don't like it,' he decided finally. 'Dead alive. From what you had to say Ena, I expected something much better. I've never been here before, remember. I wasn't particularly interested in your mother's crazy brother.'

'He wasn't crazy, Dad,' Ena objected. 'A — a bit *queer*, perhaps, but I think he was rather clever really. He was an entomologist, or something.'

'I know — a bug-hunter. How much longer are you going to be with that key, Nick?'

Nick was saved from answering as at that moment the ancient lock clicked back. He swung the solid teak door inward upon the dark expanse of hall. A

4

musty odour drifted slowly out. The place smelled dry, peculiar, and un-lived in.

'All we need now is Boris Karloff,' Nick grinned. 'And if you'll pardon my manners, Ena, I'll go in first — just in case the bogey-man gets you.'

'Nettles and dead sticks,' Ena's father growled, surveying the grounds. 'Trust nettles to keep on growing even in the autumn. And if anybody thinks *I'm* going to get this wilderness to rights they can think again!'

He realized suddenly that he was talking to himself, so he hurried through the dim hall, catching a glimpse of armoury and brass shields as he went, and finally came upon Nick and Ena in an enormous lounge. It had weather-dirty French windows, an immensely high ceiling; panelled wall; and an old-fashioned oil lamp cluster in the central panel overhead. What afternoon light there was left fell upon costly antique furniture, an old bookcase, stuffed on every shelf, rich quality carpet, and skin rugs. Finally there was a huge old-style fireplace.

'Furnished!' Ena exclaimed at last,

astonished. 'I never thought of that! How ridiculous our never-never goods and chattels are going to look amongst this.'

Nick laughed a little. 'There's a lot of things which you never seem to think of, darling. You accepted this bequest on the strength of a childhood memory; it never dawned on you that it might have the furniture still in it — even though the will did talk cheerfully about appurtenances and all things thereto belonging — and now we've paid a small fortune to have our own furniture brought here as well. Bless you. You'll never be a business woman.'

'No reason why I should be with you to keep me.'

Nick kissed the end of Ena's pert little nose and then held her for a moment. They were both still in the early twenties, and only six months married. Prepared for a more or less humdrum life in a suburb, since Nick was production manager in an engineering firm in London, this bequest had come as a sudden delightful surprise. Or was it? Ena still could not make up her mind.

'I'll see what there is elsewhere,' her

father said, and took his departure. Since he was retired and, by force of circumstances, lived with his daughter, he tried as much as possible to keep to himself. He was not a believer in pushing himself into the young folks' lives.

'We can make something of the place,' Nick decided presently, considering.

'We hope.'

Ena was plainly uneasy. It was in the glances of her blue eyes, the uncertain movements of her slender body. She was a reasonably pretty blonde but not gifted with a great deal of thoughtfulness. To her, Nick was the be-all and end-all of her existence, which threw all responsibilities on his shoulders.

He was capable of taking them. Nearly six feet tall and muscled like an athlete — a hangover of his earlier days when he had been a keen sportsman — it was hardly likely an old house would worry him. Certainly his good-humoured face did not appear troubled. There was laughter in his grey eyes and a profound contempt for spooks in his firmly cut mouth.

'Maybe we should try and get a woman in to clean,' he said finally, but Ena shook her head.

'I'm still young enough to do my own hard work, and I mean to. All the place needs is brightening up . . . Only I do wish it hadn't such a gloomy look!'

'Maybe the Autumn twilight,' Nick decided. 'I'll see if there's any oil in these lamps.'

He began to get on the move. The lamps were bone-dry, he discovered, but in one of the many outhouses he found a drum of lamp oil and so spent the next hour until complete darkness had come filling up all the lamps throughout the great place. Towards six o'clock the yellow glow was spreading to every corner of the rambling old place. The effect, though, was even more disconcerting than shadowy daylight. Big areas were left without illumination.

'What do we do for food?' Ena's father asked, as he came into the room at the close of his house-survey. 'I've looked everywhere and there isn't a bite to eat, or anything to drink, except water. There's an oil stove, though, if we want to be primitive.'

'We don't *want* to be, we just can't help it,' Ena told him. 'Stuck right out here we've no gas or electricity laid on. As for food, there's some packed in the furniture van if they'd only hurry up.'

'Probably can't find the darned place,' Nick said cheerfully, bundling some rubbish into the fireplace preparatory to making a fire. 'At least we can keep warm. Three outhouses are filled with coal and logs . . . '

He broke off as somewhere an ancient bell clanged, echoing through the house. Ena jumped up from the big settee.

'That'll be the furniture men,' She said quickly, 'I'll see to them.'

She hurried from the room, picking up a portable oil lamp as she went so as to find her way across the hall She opened the front door eagerly.

'Everything's ready to be — ' she began, and then she checked herself with a little gasp of surprise. It was not the removers. In fact the man on the top step could not possibly have looked more unlike a furniture remover.

He was small, no more than five feet tall, with an enormous beaked nose, on the top of which were perched dense-lensed eyeglasses. He was wearing a black, sloppy brimmed hat and cape, this latter caught loosely at his throat with a silver chain. His hands were encased in close-fitting black gloves and the right hand gripped the silver knob of an ebony walking stick.

'Good evening,' he greeted, and raised his hat.

Ena noticed for a moment that his hair was dark as midnight and shone with amazing polish in the oil light. Not that this fascinated her particularly. It was the voice that was so impressive — smooth, mellow as syrup, a delight to hear.

'Oh — er — good evening.' Ena recovered herself. 'I — I think there must be some mistake —'

'Oh, surely not?' Even white teeth gleamed in a smile. 'I am your neighbour — the nearest, I live in the house on the hill. You must have seen it.'

Ena remembered it and nodded quickly.

'I am Dr. Lexton,' the visitor explained. 'Dr. Adam Lexton. May I have a few words with you and your husband?'

'I — I see.' Ena stood back. 'Do come in, Dr. Lexton.'

He entered the hall, removing his hat to reveal again that polished hair. Ena looked at him with vague misgivings, suddenly feeling thankful she was not alone in the house and then led the way into the lounge. Her father and Nick who were busy getting the fire to blaze, looked up in some astonishment at the visitor. In the somewhat brighter light of the several oil lamps his small stature was more noticeable, and he walked with a pronounced stoop — not so much from any apparent weakness but as though it were part of his natural figure.

'Dr. Lexton,' Ena introduced, putting down the lamp. 'He is our neighbour from up on the hill.'

There were handshakes, more surprised glances, then at Nick's invitation Lexton sat down in the armchair. He adjusted his thick glasses on his protruding beak of a nose and his tiny, minimised eyes looked sharply from one to the other.

'I — I do not wish to come here in the role of a scare-monger,' he said, 'but I feel it my duty to warn you that you would be safer in leaving this house.'

'Leave it!' Nick exclaimed. 'But we only just got here.'

'I am aware of that, Mr. Hansley. In my house I have a study on the top floor that overlooks the countryside, and I saw your car arrive this afternoon. I decided to come over right away and caution you. This is a house of danger, and death. It can do none of you any good to stop in it.'

'What's the matter with it?' asked Ena's father bluntly. 'Haunted or something?'

'One might call it that. It is dominated by an evil power.'

'I'm afraid that I for one, cannot credit that, Dr. Lexton,' Ena remarked, with a serious little smile. 'My uncle, from whom I inherited this house, was certainly a little strange in his ways, but I am sure that he did nothing that could leave a — dangerous evil power behind.'

'I was a great friend of your uncle, Mrs. Hansley,' Lexton answered. 'He was a brilliantly clever man — and certainly one of the country's foremost entomologists. But before he died he performed an experiment, which, despite his death, can still have disastrous effects on all of you. That is why I insist you should leave.'

'What kind of experiment?' Nick enquired. 'Something to do with butter-flies?'

Lexton looked up sharply. Just for a moment there was an indescribably malignancy on his pointed face; then he relaxed and gave a tolerant smile.

'I see you are a sceptic, Mr. Hansley. The experiment was concerned with entomological science. I am not in a position to give you the details. I can only warn you to leave . . . I would be prepared to buy this house from you.'

'Well, I — ' Ena began, her face brightening, but Nick cut her short.

'If there is danger in this house for us, it would also exist for you, doctor. Without wishing to sound impolite, what exactly is your little game?'

'Game?' Lexton laughed softly. 'None at all. It so happens that I have the power to defeat this evil presence, chiefly because I am a student of the occult. You have no such protection. For the sum of, say, a hundred thousand pounds, I would take this house off your hands. That is a good offer for a place so remote and bereft of amenities.'

Ena gave Nick a hopeful look, but she only saw his dogged profile. He looked as if he were trying to wrestle with something; trying to understand.

'It's a good offer,' Ena's father said, musing.

'Too good,' Nick growled. 'You've an angle in this, Dr. Lexton, otherwise you wouldn't be so desperately anxious to move in.'

Lexton was silent for a moment or two, then he rose to his feet. Picking up one of the oil lamps from the nearby sideboard he moved across to the French windows and opened them.

'Forgive a little demonstration,' he apologized, 'but I think you ought to witness the kind of power which is dominant in and around this house. Might I ask you to come here for a moment?'

Puzzled, but willing, Nick, Ena, and her father all complied, standing round Lexton's little figure as he held forth the oil lamp. Its yellow glow cast on a bed of autumn tinted nettles just in front of the French window.

'Watch,' he instructed.

Convinced they were having dealings with a crank the three gazed at the nettles intently, wondering what was due to happen next. When it did happen it was so abrupt and unbelievable it left them gasping. For, without warning, the whole bed of nettles suddenly fell flat, apparently cut off from the ground up.

'You observe?' Dr. Lexton asked quietly, then he led the way back into the lounge and set down the lamp.

Slowly the three turned away from the open window and came to where Lexton was standing. He was studying them through his dense eyeglasses.

'That was not a fake, or a conjuring trick, or something worked up for a sensation,' he explained deliberately. 'It was the influence of evil power which I, as

15

an intermediary, brought into momentary activity.'

'Meaning you are a force for evil?' Ena asked uneasily.

'No, Mrs. Hansley. I fight evil wherever I can, and my very opposition inflames it to activity. You have seen the force that exists around you and from it will have gathered the danger threatening for yourselves. So, think it over. I will return tomorrow and see if you are in any way more willing to sell this house.'

With that he took his departure, Nick seeing him to the front door. When he came back into the lounge Nick found Ena and her father just coming in through the open French window with bunches of drooping nettles in their hands.

'Queerest trick I ever saw,' Ena declared, as her father locked the French windows. 'Not a nettle standing in the whole bed. Doesn't seem to be any explanation, either. These nettles look as though they've been broken off.'

Nick took the bunch she was holding and held it close to the light of the oil lamp. There was no doubt that the stems had been smashed through on a level with the ground, though how on earth it had been done remained a mystery.

'Oh, damn the man!' Nick snapped finally, flinging the nettles in the fire. 'He pulled some kind of an illusion just to scare us — and it's not coming off. Truth is, there must be something much more valuable in, or about, this house than we ever thought of, Lexton knows about it because he was a close friend of your Uncle Cyrus, Ena — so I think the best thing we can do is look around for something interesting.'

'The only thing that interests me is something to eat and drink,' Ena's father complained. 'I wonder how the devil much longer those furniture men are — '

A ringing at the front door bell interrupted him. Instantly he got on the move, half expecting it was the peculiar Dr. Lexton back again. His guess was wrong. A burly man in a worn suit and a green baize apron stood on the step and behind him were the lights of the furniture van.

'Took some finding, this blasted place,' he complained. 'What do you want in first?'

So for the next hour at least, with the mundane job of furniture arranging to see to, Dr. Lexton and his bed of nettles was completely forgotten. Once the furniture had been fixed a meal followed, and towards ten o'clock, the trio began to feel they could examine their problems with more interest.

'As I see it,' Ena's father said, 'this man Lexton is going to make himself an infernal nuisance trying to get us out of here, so we'd better all make up our minds to say 'No!' to him tomorrow and really mean it.'

'If we *do* mean it,' Ena sighed, with a glance about her. 'After all, it is about the gloomiest place ever, and it must have been something queer which killed those nettles.'

'On the other hand nobody wants to buy a weird house for a hundred thousand pounds without a strong reason,' Nick objected. 'We may be perched over oil, valuable minerals, uranium ore — or

18

there might be something in the place which is of great value. Before we go to bed I suggest a thorough search.'

'Good enough,' Ena's father agreed, rising stiffly. 'Though I have looked the place over. It apparently has dozens of well-furnished bedrooms, four bathrooms, and apart from this lounge there is a library, music room, dining room, and kitchen regions. What one man could want with such a place is beyond me! Anyway, I'll look through the library as a likely spot for something interesting; you two examine the other rooms.'

With that he wandered out of the lounge and across the hall, picking up the oil lamp in the hall on his way. Once in the great, cold library he set down the lamp and drew the curtains across the vast windows. He shivered a little to himself. This mighty residence was like a tomb after the cosy warmth of the suburban home to which he had been accustomed,

Picking the lamp up again he held it over his head and examined the seemingly endless rows of books. None of them were fiction. All related to some science or other, but in the main they dealt with entomology. Since insects were the last thing in which Ena's father was interested he did not dwell too long on the titles. He moved on to the bureau and found it unlocked. But there were no papers within it. Everything had been removed leaving only an empty piece of furniture. On again to a tall case fixed in an angle of the wall. It was rather like a mummy case in shape, only bigger, and looked as though it were part of the wall itself, fitting exactly into the right angle created by the corner.

Ena's father peered at it interestedly, looking for some Egyptian symbols — and finding none. Finally he began to investigate for some way of opening the vertical lid. In so doing he evidently hit a concealed spring for the lid shot open abruptly, narrowly missing his face.

He held up the oil lamp and then gave a gasp of horror. He had seen many weird things in his life, even terrifying things, but none of them had equalled this. With a gasp he swung away and blundered back across the library and into the hall.

'Ena!' he shouted hoarsely. 'Ena! Nick! Come *here*!'

He was so startled the oil lamp was quivering in his grip. He was still perspiring and breathing hard when Nick and Ena came clattering down the stairs from investigating the upper regions.

'What is it, Dad?' Ena asked in concern. 'You look scared to death.'

'Not — not scared. Just bowled over. Come and look at this.'

Ena followed her father back into the library, Nick coming up in the rear. When they stared at the object in the case they recoiled for a moment, but sheer fascination kept them looking at it.

It resembled a gigantic wasp standing upright. In the light it was all of nine feet, possessing stalked eyes and triple rows of teeth. The body was chitinous, the head massive, and coarse hair covered the legs.

'What the devil *is* it?' Ena's father demanded. 'It's enough to give a man of my age heart failure! I know your Uncle Cyrus was an insect-collector, Ena, but where did he find this one? It doesn't resemble anything I ever saw before, not

21

even in a natural history book.'

'Looks like a cross between a wasp and an ant,' Nick said, going closer. 'Queer colour too — a sort of blood-red. Nearest thing I think of resembling it is the red ant, though no red ant was ever this size.'

'Cleverly stuffed,' Ena said, plucking up the courage to move to Nick's side so she could examine the thing with more detail.

'This isn't stuffed,' Nick said after a while, wonder in his voice. 'Believe it or not it has been built up piece by piece from the original creature — just as prehistoric monsters are built up in the museum.'

There was silence for a moment. The thought that such a hideous and gigantic insect could possibly have once existed was sobering. Had it been alive it could easily have dealt with the three surveying it now.

'Maybe this is what Lexton wants,' Ena's father suggested, and Nick gave a start.

'Could be, Dad. I never thought of it. Wish I had more idea what this thing is, though. It may be valuable.'

'Valuable!' Ena exclaimed. 'A horrible thing like this!'

'Science, dear one, sometimes pays a fortune for what looks like an Irish stew bone, just because it is a missing piece in a vital fossil. What would science pay, perhaps, for a complete insect like this, utterly outside known classification . . . ? I think,' Nick went on, musing, 'that I might do worse than ask Len Chalmers to come down here.'

'Len?' Ena repeated, then she remembered. 'Oh, you mean that friend of yours who is an animal illustrator?'

'He's more than that. Because of his work as an animal, bird, and insect artist he has to know every type of insect there is. He might know this one. No harm in asking him to take a look. I'd call and see him personally only I have my fortnight's vacation to finish and I don't see any reason for spoiling it by driving up to London. Besides, I want to choke Lexton off when he comes again.'

'For the moment I think we'll shut the lid on this thing,' Ena's father said, and he did so with vehement satisfaction.

Then he turned and asked, 'Either of you find anything worthwhile anywhere else?'

'Nothing,' Nick answered, 'but we may as well go on searching until bed-time. Then I'll put the car in the garage and we may as well call it a day.'

They all left the library together, but though they spent the rest of the evening investigating they failed to discover anything of outstanding interest. Their thoughts naturally turned back to the strange Dr. Lexton and the incredible object in the library case.

Nick and Ena were still discussing it from all angles when they retired to bed, and in his own room Ena's father sat musing and smoking his pipe. He had come to the conclusion he did not like The Cedars one little bit. It had been much better at the other home with the pub only a few yards down the road . . .

# 2

## The thing in the case

The house did not seem quite so desolate or frightening next morning, perhaps because bright autumn sunlight through the great windows lent a more cheerful air to things.

Nick went to the village early to pick up some food and other supplies, and to telephone his friend Len Chalmers, enlisting his help. Quickly he gave the main details, and Chalmer's was immediately interested, promising to arrive that afternoon. His own car was in for repair, but he could catch a train to the village. Inquiry at the station told Nick that the next train out of London was due to arrive around four in the afternoon.

On his return to the house Nick helped Ena in the task of getting things to rights. There were a hundred and one things to do to remove the traces of Uncle Cyrus and make the domicile fit for the new owners.

Then, towards four that afternoon, Nick went to the station in the car to meet his friend — finding him just the same as ever. Chalmers was thirty-five, intensely serious, a brilliant artist, and a keen thinker. But for his paramount love of art he could probably have been an outstanding scientist for there were few scientific angles on which he could not discourse at length.

In appearance he was tall and thin with a tendency to frontal baldness. As he was driven from the station along the country lanes he listened attentively to the story Nick had to tell. He did not smile once: if he did anything at all he frowned. Nor did he commit himself.

'Have to see what the thing looks like,' was his only comment, but he looked unusually thoughtful just the same,

As the car came over the rise his gaze wandered to the distant solitary hill where the residence of Dr. Lexton stood, visible in the bright sunlight as a yellow-walled dwelling of extremely queer design. It had never struck Nick before but now he came to notice it the building did not seem to have any chimneys.

Then the trees hid it from sight and The Cedars came into view. Five minutes later Len was shaking hands with Ena and her father.

'The more people there are in this house the better I like it,' Ena said, glancing about her. 'It's so huge and gloomy and frightening. I'd like to sell out to Dr. Lexton and get back to the city, but Nick won't hear of it.'

'Not yet anyway,' Nick responded. 'I think we should find out why Lexton is willing to give one hundred thousand for a place as isolated as this.'

'Anyway, Mr. Chalmers, come and have something to eat,' Ena's father invited. 'It's all ready for you in the dining room — '

'Kind of you, sir, but later,' Len smiled. 'I had a good lunch and it is only quarter past four as yet. I'm all anxiety to see this mystery insect of yours.'

'Not *ours*!' Ena shuddered. 'I wouldn't own it!'

Nick led the way across the hall and into the library. He had to fish for a while until he found the spring to the case — then the lid shot to one side and the weird insect was revealed in the low shafts of sunlight through the window.

Len Chalmers did not look startled — only interested. His sandy eyebrows went up and a thoughtful look came in his blue eyes. He advanced slowly and inspected the object closely. Then at last he shook his head.

'No, I don't know what it is,' he confessed. 'It doesn't fall into anything of the prehistoric genus, either.'

'I get the idea it has been built up from the original parts of the insect,' Nick remarked. 'Think I'm right?'

'Quite right — which is what makes it so strange. It must have existed to commence with to have been built up. Basically I think it is a type of red ant, but of huge size. Notice the faceted eyes, the chitinous body, the mandibles. It has all the characteristics of a red neuter, yet in many ways it is different. Hanged if I can understand it.'

28

'Did you tell Len about the nettles, Nick?' Ena asked.

'Yes, he did,' Len replied, turning away from the case. 'I'd rather like to have a look at that nettle bed. But please remember I'm no detective.'

'You're a scientist of sorts,' Nick said, smiling, 'and that's good enough for us.'

With Len beside him he left the library, Ena following on behind, Her father remained, smoking his pipe and looking at the hideous insect in the case — then he slammed the lid on it impatiently. He had just turned away from it when something happened. He didn't know *what* for it was beyond comprehension.

Suddenly he found himself looking at something gigantic and shadowy, something just like the thing in the case — only this one was alive and moving. It was not standing upright but horizontal, on its six bent legs. Its stalked, terrible eyes were waving, its rows of teeth bared.

Ena's father stared at it in frozen horror, dimly conscious of the fact that he could see the library walls *through* the apparition; then sheer panic overwhelming him he made for the door. As he went he found his mind drowning in a sea of evil. He thought of things obscene, saw visions like those of hell itself. A ghastly nausea welled up within him and sent him reeling as he crossed the hall.

He reached the lounge doorway and saw Nick, Ena, and Len beyond the French windows at the nettle bed — then his strength failed him. He called weakly and sank down, his mind drowning in darkness.

When he came to again he was lying on the settee with the bitter after-taste of brandy in his mouth. Blearily he looked at his daughter, then to the grim faces of Nick and Len.

'What happened, Dad?' Ena asked in alarm. 'Did — did you have a heart attack or something?'

'No . . . ' He moved slowly. 'No! My heart's as good as yours, my girl, even if it is thirty years older. I — I saw something. A ghost of the thing in the case. Then I got to thinking of things the basest criminals would think of — and maybe not even them . . . '

'What on Earth do you mean?' Nick demanded. 'Dad, talk sense! What *happened*?'

Ena's father gave the story as it had occurred. When it was over he was practically himself again, though badly shaken. Len Chalmers had a faraway look in his eyes.

'I begin to think,' Ena said slowly, 'that Dr. Lexton was right when he spoke of an evil presence.'

'Oh, rubbish!' Len Chalmers was unusually emphatic. 'It was nothing occult which affected your father: it was something which has a scientific explanation if only I could find it. For instance, one might say that those nettles fell flat because of psychic power, yet nothing could be further from the truth. Just before your collapse, sir,' he added, looking at Ena's father, 'I had discovered that the nettles fell because they had been bitten through.'

'Bitten!' Nick gave a start. 'But — but bitten by *what*?'

'Insects of some sort. My mind strays

31

naturally to neuter ants which have powerful mandibles.'

Ena's father sat up slowly, his face blank.

'Why in the name of sanity should ants want to bite through a bed of nettles?' he demanded. 'If it comes to that, how *could* they? It just doesn't make sense.'

'I know it doesn't — off hand. But I'm commencing to think of all sorts of possibilities. There's certainly far more going on in this house, and around it, than any of us realize.' Len considered for a moment and then asked a question. 'Do you know, Ena, if your uncle had any way of making insects do his bidding?'

'I've not the slightest idea,' Ena replied blankly. 'All I knew about Uncle was that he was an entomologist, but what he actually did in connection with insects I don't know . . . In any case, Len, I can't see what you are driving at. Even supposing he *did* have some kind of influence over insects, it couldn't apply now, could it? He's dead.'

Len sighed. 'I'm trying to find a link,' he explained, 'There is some sort of tie-up between that thing in the case, the nettles which were destroyed, your father's weird delusion a little while ago, and Dr. Lexton. They all fit into a pattern somewhere, but I just can't seem to — '

Len paused and glanced up as there was a ringing at the front door bell. Ena straightened from the settee and gave Nick a glance.

'Probably Lexton come for an answer,' she said. 'We'll soon tell *him*!'

'Don't scare him away,' Len warned. 'I want to meet him.'

Ena nodded and left the room. Presently she returned with Dr. Lexton following behind her, hat, stick, and gloves in his left hand. His teeth gleamed as he gave a welcoming smile and shook hands with the men. Then he looked at Ena's father in surprise as he sat half slumped on the settee.

'Not feeling well, my friend?' Lexton enquired in concern.

'Father had a queer turn,' Ena answered briefly. 'And I think we can soon dispose of our business, Dr. Lexton. We have definitely decided against selling this house.'

Lexton did not betray his feelings by any change of expression. He looked about him, adjusting his heavy glasses on his huge nose. Len Chalmers was studying him intently.

'I gather,' Lexton remarked finally. 'that you are unconvinced that psychic power is at work?'

'Completely so, doctor,' Len responded. 'Quite a few strange things have been happening, including hallucinations on the part of Mrs. Hansley's father — but I for one do not believe in psychic power being the cause. I am more inclined to suspect a scientific reason.'

'You are a scientist, Mr. Chalmers?' Lexton enquired.

'A dabbler; nothing more. But there is a great deal in this business that interests me. The fact that nettles can be bitten through by insects at a given moment, for one thing; and for another a remarkable specimen in a case in the library.'

'Oh, you mean the red ant?' Lexton laughed half to himself. 'Rather hideous, is it not? Mr. Odder — Mrs. Hansley's Uncle — created that being, you know.'

Len, Nick, Ena, and her father became intent.

'Created it?' Nick repeated in surprise. 'How do you mean? Built it up, surely?'

'*Created* it,' Lexton repeated firmly. 'However, it is a matter of profound entomological surgery and I do not propose to go into it. My main regret is that you have decided against leaving. I am convinced it is a most ill-advised decision . . . However, there it is. If you ever wish to reconsider you know where my home is. Or, better still,' Lexton added, thinking, 'send me a message and I will come over and see you. I have a great dislike for visitors. They disturb my studies.'

'I'll see you to the door,' Nick volunteered — and he did not delay about it, either. When he returned into the lounge he found Len Chalmers lost in speculations and Ena making sure that her father had now completely recovered.

'Which settles him!' Nick exclaimed, rubbing his hands. 'Now where do we go from here?'

'There is something about which I should warn you,' Len said, his voice and expression serious. 'Don't try crossing Lexton's wishes too much.'

'Why not?' Ena demanded spiritedly. 'He can't tell *us* what to do, the horrible little *gnome*!'

'It's just possible that he *can*,' Len answered grimly. 'That's why I'm urging you to be careful. He is the only possible person — since your Uncle is dead — who could have control enough over insects to make them do his bidding at a given time. And it must have been done mentally. If he had that much power he might just as easily influence humans.'

'Hypnotically?' Nick questioned, frowning.

'Why not? Ena's father saw things that were not normal, didn't he? And felt mental urges right outside his usual run of thoughts.'

The brief silence was a troubled one. Then Ena said abruptly, 'Just who *is* Lexton, I wonder? What is he supposed to be? What is he a doctor of, for instance?'

'It may pay us to find out before long,' Len answered. 'In the meantime I want another look at that ant specimen. Lexton admitted quite freely that it is a giant red ant and that your Uncle Cyrus created it, Ena — so that demands a second look. It begins to appear as though your uncle experimented with some kind of insectile surgery and produced that vile-looking thing in the case.'

He hurried from the lounge and went across the hall to the library. By the time he had got the case open the others had caught up with him and stood watching as he took a spring rule from his pocket and began to measure the monster insect carefully. Halfway through the task however, he paused and frowned, peering at something behind the insect. Just at this moment the sunlight was streaming directly into the recess, illuminating it in detail.

'I'll be damned!' Len exclaimed softly, his attention completely absorbed.

'What?' Nick asked. 'Something queer?'

'I'll say! There's a panel directly behind this specimen, and from the look of it, it ought to open! Here — give me a hand to get this monster out of the way.'

Nick did not hesitate a moment. He and Len between them unfastened the wires that held the insect in position and at length they were able to carry it to the library table. From the weight of the thing it had all its internal organs correctly in place, too, which made the mystery all the more profound.

With it out of the way, and the sunlight for illumination, it became obvious that the very back of the recess was not part of the wall, but a separate slide or door. There was a hair-thin crack and no sign of a handle or spring control. Finally Len took out his penknife and put the blade into the slit, bending the blade back and forth experimentally. He was rewarded at last as, with a soft click, the panel suddenly released itself and glided to one side into a recess, moving on oiled runners. Beyond there was darkness and the musty odour of the underground.

'Now we're really getting somewhere!' Nick murmured, his eyes bright with eagerness.

'Fetch a torch, please,' Len instructed, and Ena — remembering there was one in the car — hurried off to get it. In a while she returned and handed it over.

Len waved the beam into the cobwebby gloom. A narrow tunnel was revealed, just about wide enough for two stooping people to pass along it abreast.

'What do you make of it?' Nick asked, puzzled. 'I know that old houses are renowned for passages and tunnels, but this one seems queerer than most. Why bar it with that red ant, for instance?'

'Can you think of a better way to scare anybody from looking too closely for this tunnel?' Len asked dryly.

'You mean it was put there deliberately to stop this tunnel being found?' Ena asked in surprise.

'Looks decidedly like it to me. We'd better see what this tunnel has to offer.'

Len stepped into it, flashing the torch beam in front of him. Anxious to find what was ahead, Nick, Ena, and her father came on in the rear.

It was apparently a natural tunnel, to judge from the roughness of the walls. It was unusually dry without the usual seeping of moisture and mildew associated with the underground. For half a mile it retained its narrowness and twisted and turned considerably — then it widened out abruptly into a fair-sized cave.

'Gets more like 'Treasure Island' every minute,' Ena said excitedly — then she paused and frowned as she looked ahead. It looked for a moment as though they were the lamps of a car there, brightly lighted with a greenish tinge — but that of course was impossible.

She had no need to call the attention of the others to the incident. They had seen it, too, and halted. Then Nick gripped Len's arm tightly as there was a sudden leathery stirring in the cave and a queer sound rather like sticks being tapped vigorously against each other.

'My God — *look!*' Ena's father suddenly gasped.

Transfixed, Len, Nick, and Ena gazed at an object that had risen from the cave floor. It was all of nine feet in height and its stalked eyes were reflecting the torchlight like waving lanterns.

'It's the red ant!' Ena shrieked, stumbling backwards. 'A living edition of it . . .'

She grabbed her father's arm and

together they blundered into the tunnel up which they had come. Len and Nick stood their ground for a moment, then not being idiots they too plunged for the tunnel and gained it just as the red ant reached the opening. They could hear the leathery movements of its enormous body, the chopstick sound of its mandibles clicking — and then the sounds began to recede as, with torch beam waving wildly, they raced back along the narrow passage and into the library.

Len slammed the panel across, but it did not lock. He had evidently broken it in his efforts to release it. Breathing hard and mopping his face, he turned.

'Nice little playmate!' he commented, still looking startled.

'I just don't understand it,' Ena said breathlessly, her eyes wide. 'What in the world is that horrible thing doing down there? How does it live? What does it feed on? Think what would happen if it came up the passage and into the library here! I — I think we ought to get out right away. I have the idea Uncle Cyrus went too far with his beastly insects.'

'Or else he accomplished a miracle of entomology,' Len answered, thinking. 'We got a shock, certainly, but let's look at the thing squarely before we go off the deep end. That object down there is so big it cannot get up the narrow tunnel neck, so that leaves us in peace — or should do. It means it either grew to its present size in that cave, or else it was grown elsewhere and taken horizontally down the passage way. Doped, perhaps. Last of all, it is the exact replica of that model ant on the table there.'

Every eye looked at it. Then Ena's father said,

'But it isn't a model. It's a built-up image of the original. Which, with the one that's alive, makes two.'

'And neither of them looks like a red ant,' Len continued, thinking. 'Neither in size nor contour. They're utterly different. Gigantic specimens! The more we see the less we wonder at Dr. Lexton wanting to buy us out, or rather you . . . ' Len gave an apologetic grin. 'I keep including myself in the family, which I shouldn't.'

'Welcome, brother,' Nick said fervently.

'We need a man like you at a time like this.'

'We know,' Len continued, 'that Lexton and your Uncle Cyrus, Ena, knew each other well. I wonder if they were making an ant experiment between them when Uncle Cyrus's death brought things to a stop? I wonder, too, if the product of the experiment is that thing down underground? It would be natural for Lexton to want to continue the experiment, which he cannot do as long as this house is not his to come and go as he chooses. And, of course, he could not buy the house whilst it was Uncle Cyrus's — then it passed to you, Ena. Hmmm — it all seems to tie up in that direction.'

'But what's going *on?*' Nick demanded. 'Why the devil should anybody want to make a red ant look different and extend it to nine feet in height?'

Len gave a rather grim smile. 'Scientists, Nick, be they entomological or any other variety, are always experimenting. And in case you don't know it, the ant is really the rightful owner of this planet. Not us.'

'Ants are?' Ena's eyes went wider still.

43

'*Those* wiggly little things?'

'The ant — the whole termite colony — is the most intelligent form of life outside ourselves,' Len responded. 'We should be grateful that an accident of Nature made the ant subservient to us, otherwise — Well, I have the uneasy feeling that maybe Uncle Cyrus and Lexton between them tried to create an ant as it *should* be, then they became scared of their creation and locked it up below.'

'Where it ought to die, and doesn't,' Ena's father growled.

'An ant has a tremendous power of endurance,' Len pointed out. 'It can withstand privations which would kill a human in a fraction of the time . . . However, we're talking round a prop at the moment. What we need to do is see if we can discover any evidence to prove what Uncle Cyrus and Lexton *did* do, We'd better start searching. In here, seems a likely spot since this is where the rebuilt ant was placed.'

'A thought occurs to me,' Nick said. 'For that kind of work — entomological experiments, I mean — oughtn't there to be a surgery or something? Or maybe a laboratory? I've seen no sign of one.'

'It's a point,' Len admitted. 'Maybe there is one underground somewhere, or it is equally possible that Dr. Lexton may have such a laboratory . . . Anyhow, let's see if we can find anything.'

So they began searching, not knowing exactly what they were looking for, just as long as it provided the slenderest of clues to clear up the mystery in which they were involved. It was perhaps not surprising that it was late that night — the only break having been for a hurried meal around seven o'clock — when something finally turned up.

It was Len who found it, in the shape of a library book that had been so well used its covers were nearly falling off. Inside it there were ink notations in handwriting that Ena identified as Uncle Cyrus's, and in each instance the notes were made alongside long scientific descriptions of termites and their habits,

'Listen to this,' Len said, setting the book down on the bureau under the oil lamp. 'From *Ant Life* by T. M. Dalby: 'If the ant had only had lungs instead of mere breathing tubes I should not have written this textbook. I would have been under the domination of the termite world, and so would everybody else'.'

Ena, her father and Nick, looked at each other. Len skimmed through the pages, then quoted from another well-thumbed context.

' 'Man is perhaps a million years old: the ant is *fifty million* years old. The ant, therefore, is better organized, better disciplined, and indeed belongs to a super race which lacks only one vital thing — *lungs*'!'

'All very interesting, but where does it get us?' Nick questioned.

Len put the book down, his face thoughtful. 'The ant,' he said, 'has no lungs at all. Only breathing tubes. Therefore, every time the ant has tried to grow bigger it has failed because of breathing apparatus. But suppose it was equipped with breathing apparatus — lungs? How then?'

There was stunned silence for a moment; then Ena started.

'Great heavens, you mean that maybe that — that thing in the cave is how an ant would look if it could breathe like you or me?'

'That's what I'm thinking,' Len admitted. 'It's not only a sobering thought: it's a dangerous one. If that ant happens to have sex — not a neuter that is — and there is any other ant anywhere of similar dimensions and the opposite sex almost anything can happen. Ants that size could give humanity a desperate run for their money.'

'Apparently,' Nick said slowly, 'we've stumbled on something mighty big. I think we ought to go and see Lexton, tell him what we have discovered, and demand an explanation.'

'Before we do I want more information,' Len decided. 'I am going to take this ant specimen to the Institute of Entomology in London and get the best possible brains to pass an opinion. I am also taking some of those dead nettles. They are still capable of being analysed even though they have withered. On whatever findings I get, I'll act — and if

Lexton is up to something we'll have the law on him mighty quickly. In any case something has to be done about that monster in the cellar. We might make arrangements to have it shot or gassed — but on the other hand the Entomology Institute might prefer to take it away for examination, much as big game hunters catch wild animals.'

Len made up his mind as he glanced at his watch. 'I'll leave for London right away,' he finished. 'I can be there by midnight and visit the Institute first thing in the morning, Give me a hand to get this horrible thing to your car. Nick — if you don't mind loaning me your car for the trip that is?'

'Welcome,' Nick replied promptly. 'Anything as long as we get some action. And let's hope this ant will fit the car!'

# 3

## Murder

Three very puzzled and not at all comfortable people were left behind once Len had departed. They did not speak much to each other. They kept thinking of that diabolical insect far under the ground, and each in turn wondered if it might have the intelligence to lie flat, wriggle along the tunnel, and to make its way into the library past the insecurely fastened wall slide. All they could do, since it was obviously not possible to desert the house and so play into Dr. Lexton's hands was take that chance.

Ena's father was the first to announce his intention of retiring — not with any great enthusiasm. The thought of the lonely corridors and big, old-fashioned rooms, was disturbing to him. Nonetheless he took his good night of the two younger people with as much cheerfulness as he could muster and left the lounge. Nick and Ena remained near the fire, whither they had moved after supper.

'It looks to me, Ena, as though we — '

Nick had just started to say something when he was interrupted by a scream. It echoed in the cavernous reaches of the house and was followed by a series of heavy bumps and, finally, one extra loud one. By this time Ena had flown to the door, snatching up an oil lamp on her way. Nick came racing behind her.

'Dad!' Ena cried hoarsely, pointing. 'Dad, what's happened?'

She fled across the hall to the base of the huge staircase. Her father's huddled figure was lying there, hands outflung as he had tried to save himself. Nearby the oil lamp he had been carrying was flooding burning oil along the parquet flooring. Nick snatched his overcoat from the hallstand and flung it on the flames, smothering them. Then he moved over to where Ena was crouched, supporting her father's head and shoulders in her arm.

'He's — he's — ' She could not get the words out. Emotion choked her.

Nick looked at the white face and staring eyes pillowed against the girl's breast, then he took her father's wrist and felt for the pulse. It was no longer beating.

'He's — dead,' Ena whispered, tears streaming down her cheeks. 'He — he must have fallen down the stairs or something. Oh, Nick — *Nick!*'

For the next ten minutes Nick had his hands full. With some difficulty he carried the body upstairs to the bedroom and covered the sheet over it; then he had to return to the lounge and do his best to comfort the nearly hysterical girl.

'We've no guarantee that he just slipped and killed himself!' she insisted. 'I think it was something else. Remember that awful scream he gave. Dad wasn't the type to do that without a very real reason . . .'

'Look, Ena — try and calm yourself for a moment.' Nick took hold of her quivering shoulders firmly. 'Horrible though this sudden tragedy is, particularly for you since he was your father, we've got certain technicalities to think of.'

'Technicalities?' Ena looked at him dumbly.

'Certainly. We've go to report the matter. There will doubtless be a coroner's inquest. At the very least I've got to find a local doctor. Since Len has the car and we've no 'phone the only solution is to walk to the village — '

'Not without me,' Ena said urgently, jumping up. 'I'm not going to be left alone here, Nick! I'm not, I tell you.'

'I wouldn't wish it,' he assured her quietly. 'Get on your things and we'll get moving. If Lexton is watching our movements, then let him. I hardly think he will be because had he wanted to break into this house he could have done it long ago, before we took up residence here.'

Ena was too dazed with grief to pay much attention. She went out into the hall and scrambled into her hat and coat. Nick did likewise then, together, they left the gloomy pile and went down the drive. It was a good two miles to the village but the prospect was not very appalling. It was almost a relief to get away from the sombre environs of The Cedars.

'Hello!' Nick exclaimed suddenly, as they turned a bend in the lane. 'Car broken down, or something.'

Ena looked moodily ahead of her. To one side of the lane was a car's rear light. She thought nothing of it for the moment until she realized that the number plate — visible as the distance narrowed — belonged to Nick's car.

'That's odd,' Nick said, recognizing the number plate at the same moment. 'Where the devil's Len got to?'

He hurried forward with Ena beside him and in a moment or two they had reached the car. There was no trace of Len within. The ignition keys were missing, however, which seemed to suggest he had departed of his own accord. The ant was still in position.

'What on earth goes on?' Nick demanded impatiently, having had more than his share of shocks for one night. Then he raised his voice and called loudly, *'Len! Len! Are you anywhere around?'*

There was a momentary pause, then

there came an answering shout in Len's unmistakable clipped voice.

'I'm here — in the wood! Follow my voice!'

Nick and Ena looked in wonder at the thick trees dimly visible in the darkness at the side of the lane. Since Len kept calling to give them direction they scrambled up the bank, plunged through the undergrowth, and finally came upon Len in the midst of a thicket. He struck up his almost exhausted cigarette lighter,

'Nice thing I've discovered!' he exclaimed, his tone showing he was both baffled and startled. His face too was greasy, either from exertion or excitement.

'Len — Dad's . . . dead,' Ena said, straight out, and then she found she couldn't say any more. She had started to cry again.

The lighter expired. 'Dead?' came Len's appalled voice from the gloom. 'But — but how? What happened?'

'He fell down stairs, I think,' Nick responded, and gave the details. 'We were on our way to find a doctor and report the matter when we saw the car.'

'That's damnable,' Len muttered. 'I just can't be sorry enough, Ena — though words are cheap, I suppose.'

'And you?' Nick asked, trying to keep the situation in focus. 'What have you happened on that's so important?'

'I don't know what to make of it,' Len answered. 'I was driving down the lane from The Cedars when my headlights swept across this neck of the woods. Just for a moment, clear as day, I saw our little friend Dr. Lexton. I had just time to notice that he was digging like fury at this spot. I gathered he was startled by my lights for he looked up sharply, and by that time I'd swung past. Just the same I pulled up further down the lane and came into the wood here. I heard footsteps running away — presumably Lexton's. This is what I found here.'

Len struck up his temporarily revived lighter and held it downwards. The yellow glimmer danced for a moment over a half buried body, without a coffin. Then the light went out again. Quickly Nick pulled out his own lighter and struck it. The brighter flame revealed a corpse that had not been lying long in the ground, but the features were unfamiliar. From the mark round his neck it looked as though he had been strangled.

'Obviously,' came Len's grim voice, as the lighter expired, 'Lexton knows about this. I think he was trying to dig the body up when I interrupted him. I get the impression he never expected nosy strangers in his territory and, having failed to buy you out, he's trying to cover up the traces of some crime.'

'We've got to get action,' Nick decided. 'I'll stay here by this body while you go and inform the police. You can either stay here with me, Ena, or if you feel more comfortable away from this corpse then go with Len. And get a doctor.'

'I'll — I'll stay here,' came her weary, frightened voice, and with that Len hurried away through the wood. When at last there was the sound of the car moving away towards the village Ena spoke again.

'Nick, what is the explanation of this terrible business? The monstrous red ant — the reconstructed one in the back of your car — the death of poor Dad, and now this? Do — do you think Lexton is a homicidal maniac or something?'

'Certainly something, Ena, though I would hesitate to call him a homicidal maniac. He's up to some dire, deep game, and the only people who can deal with him are the police.'

Ena fell silent. She was overcome again by thoughts of her dead father and did not arouse herself until there were sounds of feet crashing through the undergrowth and powerful torches came into view. Finally a police inspector, sergeant, and a constable had arrived, with Len and another man in the background.

Nick and Ena watched in silence. The man behind Len went down into the shallow grave and examined the corpse in the flood of light; then he climbed out again.

'Manual strangulation,' he said briefly. 'If there's anything else I won't know till I've made a post mortem. The body had better be removed to the mortuary at Clancester. I can examine it there . . . I'm Dr. Andrews,' he continued, as he saw Nick looking at him. 'I understand you require me, Mr. — er — '

'Hansley,' Nick said. 'My father-in-law died in somewhat peculiar circumstances earlier tonight. I'd like you to come back with me to The Cedars.'

'Very well.'

'You know who this poor devil is, doctor?' the inspector asked, as the corpse was dragged from its crude resting place.

'Dr. Royd,' the medico answered. 'I recognized him immediately. He's been dead about three days near as I can tell.'

There was an interval of note-taking and Nick looked from one to the other.

'What happens now?' he enquired. 'Do you want us to go to the police station with you, inspector?'

'No, sir, that won't be necessary. Mr. Chalmers has given us a statement upon which we can act. We'll call and have a word with Dr. Lexton regarding this business. But I would like you to call in at the station tomorrow morning and tell me what you know of Lexton.'

'Since I know so little of him I can do that now,' Nick responded. 'He's tried to buy The Cedars from my wife and I

— and we refused to sell. That's all we know.' He paused, a little puzzled. 'But surely he's known in the district, inspector? Why ask me about him?'

'He's a comparative stranger,' the inspector replied. 'In fact I think he only took up residence about the time Mr. 'Cyrus' Odder died. Maybe a little later than that. Can't be more than three months ago. I've seen him now and again, knocking about. In fact he called one day to ask where he could get permission to have alterations made to that place he's got on the hill . . . Anyway, I think we should have a talk with him — and soon.'

'Who is this Dr. Royd who's been strangled?' Len asked, thinking.

'Well known doctor around here, sir — or was.' The inspector thought for a moment. 'Brain surgeon. He has quite a large exclusive practice in Clancester, the nearest town to here. People used to come even from London to consult him. Not very long ago he informed the police that he was leaving home for a while and asked us to keep an eye on his place — which we did. Naturally, his absence was not questioned. That he should be found here, like this, is the devil of a shock.'

There was a puzzled interval, then Nick stirred.

'Well, since there is nothing more to be done we'll get back to The Cedars. I take it you know about the red ant, Inspector?'

'Mmmm — the what?' The inspector was plainly surprised.

'Nothing, Inspector,' Len said quietly. 'Mr. Hansley is only referring to that model insect in the car.'

'Oh, that! Horrible-looking thing. Sooner you sell it to the Entomology Institute the better, I should say.'

Nick was about to argue the point but he felt the compulsion of Len's hand. So, with Ena between them and the doctor to the rear they returned to the lane. There were three cars lined up in the lane — Nick's own, the doctor's, and the police car with its lettered sign.

'Follow us, Doc,' Nick said, and settled at the driving seat. Ena took the front seat next to him, her head ducked low to avoid the upthrusting ant which had its vile head pushed through the open sunshine roof. Len took what remained of the back seat.

'What's the idea?' Nick demanded, as he got the car under way. 'About this infernal ant, I mean? Didn't you tell the inspector all the facts? Concerning that thing in the underground passage, for instance?'

'No, I thought better of it. I had to explain this thing in the car, so I said I had been on my way to the Entomological Institute in London when I happened on Lexton in the wood. I'm keeping quiet about that ant in the underground for the moment. We may have stumbled on a tremendous scientific secret — or achievement — and I don't want the police ruining everything with questions, notebooks, and hidebound procedure generally.'

'I hope you haven't forgotten that that horrible ant is liable to walk in on us some day,' Ena put in.

'I'm aware of it, but since it has not done so up to now I don't think it will. I believe it is too big to get up that narrow tunnel neck — even long-wise. Anyway, I've another angle for the moment. I want to ask you a question concerning your Uncle, Ena. Did you attend his funeral?'

'Attend it!' Ena echoed. 'I *arranged* it! I was uncle's only living relative.'

'Just how did he die, Ena? Sorry to be so much of a nuisance but I've got a theory buzzing round in my head. You've time to tell me before we reach The Cedars.'

'He was found dead just outside the gates of The Cedars by a passer-by. He was dressed in his outdoor clothes and had evidently had heart failure whilst out walking. The police were told. In his wallet was a ready-written letter saying that, as he was aware his heart was not too good, he might drop dead at any moment. If so, communication must be made with me, and his solicitors. The police informed me. Uncle's letter also asked that his body be conveyed to my home for burial — beside his sister, my mother — in a southeast London cemetery. Everything he asked for was done and afterwards I inherited his house and a fair sum of money. I never saw The Cedars until I arrived to take over with poor Dad, and Nick.'

'Convenient sort of death, somehow,' Len commented. 'What was the doctor's report?'

'Heart failure. Uncle was not a young man, you know.'

Len did not say what he was thinking. In fact he did not have the chance for The Cedars had been reached and Nick drew up at the front door. He alighted and the doctor also emerged from his own car to the rear. In a matter of perhaps five minutes Nick, Ena, and Len were waiting in the lounge whilst Andrews examined the body upstairs. After a while he came to make his report.

'Syncope,' he said, shrugging, as Ena looked at him questioningly. 'His heart was not in particularly good shape, anyway.'

Ena did not say anything. She looked as though she did not believe the verdict for a moment.

'Then we can proceed with burial?' Nick asked. 'There does not need to be a coroner's inquest?'

'No. Death was occasioned by natural causes — to the best of my belief.'

Andrews finished writing out his certificate and left it on the table, then he excused himself and departed.

'It's not true!' Ena insisted. 'I'm convinced of it — Dad was far too full of life to just pass out in that fashion. I think there is more behind it.'

'Possibly — but right at this moment we can't prove it,' Nick responded. 'Have to accept the verdict, I'm afraid, and first thing tomorrow I'll make the funeral arrangements . . . How about you, Len? What's the next move?'

'I'm going to London as I originally planned,' he replied. 'I'll be back again during tomorrow with, I hope, a few opinions. I've got a rather remarkable notion concerning Dr. Lexton, but before I express it, I want all the corroborative evidence I can get. If my guess is right . . . '

He paused, plunged into speculations.

'I fancy the police will take care of him, anyway,' Nick said.

'Perhaps. On the other hand he may be more than a match for them. For the moment, though, I'm attending to our own troubles — so I'll be on my way.'

And at about this time the local Inspector with his stolid sergeant behind him was hammering violently on the curious triangular-shaped door of Dr. Lexton's home. But there came no response from within.

'Probably asleep, sir,' the sergeant said. 'It is well after midnight.'

'Then he's got to be awakened,' the inspector snapped, and began hammering again; but still there was no sign of life or movement within the curious abode with no chimneys.

'All right, we'll force an entry,' the inspector decided finally. 'It isn't strictly legal to do so, I know, but we've got to get some action. Better see what windows we can find which can be forced.'

This did not prove a particularly difficult task for a window fronting on to the side drive opened easily enough under 'persuasion'. Heaving and grunting with exertion the sergeant clambered over the sill and dropped into a dark room beyond. The inspector followed him, then he and the sergeant looked around them in the glow of the electric torch beam.

They were in a comfortably furnished study with all the usual appointments, but there was no sign of Lexton anywhere. Nor, as the inspector and sergeant went on a tour of the house, did they find him. The bedroom had the appearance of never being used, which was quite a contrast to the remainder of the house.

'Well,' the inspector said at last, with considerable irritation, 'he either hasn't returned from the nocturnal activities at which Mr. Chalmers caught him — or else he is in this place somewhere, hiding. It wouldn't be impossible. This is one of the queerest-shaped houses I ever struck. More like a beehive than a house. No corners in it, domed ceilings in each room. Wonder if there's a basement?'

This got both men on the move again, but for all their searching they could find no evidence of a cellar. They could, however, hear something — yet they could not explain it. It was like a faraway whispering, like a beehive heard from a distance on a drowsy summer afternoon. It could have come from below, from above, from almost anywhere.

'I don't get it,' the inspector muttered finally. 'And it seems to me we're wasting time here. We'll put Jepson on to watch this place and have him relieved later. If Lexton is somewhere within we'll stop him getting out — and if he's out we'll stop him getting in. The minute we find him he's under arrest on suspicion of murder.'

And with that decision the inspector led the way out of the house by the open window again, and the sergeant followed him into the night. Not knowing where to look they had never even glimpsed the thin crack which indicated a panel in the hall stairway, beyond which were steps, at the foot of which was a weirdly shaped room. And in it, Dr. Adam Lexton . . .

# 4

## Dr. Lexton's secret

By the following afternoon, since Lexton had not been seen anywhere near his home, every police station in the country had been circulated with his description and every man of the law was on the lookout. P. C. Jepson had been relieved at Lexton's home and the second constable was waiting, muttering to himself, and still waiting.

Nothing happened.

It was also on the following afternoon that Len Chalmers returned from his London visit, to find that the funeral arrangements for Ena's father had been made. Len looked tired through lack of sleep, but otherwise he had a suppressed eagerness about him.

'Any luck?' Nick questioned.

'The best in the world, I think — and it supports my own theory.' Len settled in the big armchair near the fire and lighted a cigarette. 'I had the entomological experts at work. It wasn't difficult: they're glad of any excuse to air their knowledge. My first guess, that the nettles were bitten through by hordes of neuter ants, was dead right. Microscopic analysis shows that to be true.'

'And that red ant?' Ena asked quickly. 'Had they any light to throw on it?'

'Yes. It is not a genuine ant but a gigantic composite. In other words it is a combination of many types of ant all embodied in one — just as one gets a representation of a certain type of face in photography by overprinting dozens of faces and blending the characteristics into a common whole. The giant ant is nothing more than a combination of three ant types in one — male, female and neuter Originally, according to the experts, there was probably one type of ant — but with the passage of time — fifty million years remember! — the species split up into various categories, such as the white ant, black. And red. And male, female, and neuter. Combine all the types and the two sexes and neuter and you get an object like the one in the library, or like the living one in the cellar.'

'But surely ants were never *that* size?' Nick objected.

'No; that is a different thing altogether. Induced growth. And, I believe, the addition of lungs which makes the growth possible and transforms the ant from a tiny, busy, intelligent little insect into the dangerous monster we have seen.'

Nick and Ena looked at each other, each of them still mystified.

'I know what I'm talking about,' Len continued, 'and I also know something else. The giant ant — and the created one in the library — came about because of your Uncle, Ena. He and Dr. Royd, the man we found strangled, performed the experiment between them.'

'What!' Ena gasped, astounded.

'As I said before, when I came to have a look at this queer business, I am not a detective,' Len continued; 'but I hope I have my share of average intelligence. So I formed a theory — and to substantiate it, after discovering Dr. Royd's murdered body last night, I took the chance of breaking into Royd's home on my way back from London this afternoon. I knew I would be more or less safe doing so since the police are not watching it now they know Royd has been rubbed out. I wanted to see if I could find anything of interest in Royd's library, or surgery, or somewhere. I got all I wanted from a personal diary locked in his desk.'

'Locked in?' Nick repeated, horrified. 'You broke open the desk, then?'

'Yes.' Len was quite calm about it. 'I considered myself justified, because if I am right there's an appalling danger threatening — not only to you, and Ena, and me, but everybody in the world! Any liberty taken to smash that threat is reasonable . . . Anyhow, I discovered notes that verified the opinion of the entomology experts — namely that the ant of today in its many guises is only part of a much bigger and more complicated organism, a true ant. Between them, Cyrus Odder and Dr. Royd, the one a brilliant entomologist and the other a brain-surgeon, which would include anatomy in general I expect, performed an experiment. They took three ants — male, female, and neuter, and merged their characteristic strains, finally producing a hybrid from an egg. The hybrid was given synthetic lungs and grew to be like the creature that had been built up in sections in the library. That object was a sort of 'blueprint,' but made of synthetic bone and shell covering, indistinguishable at first sight from the real thing.'

'Then — then who is Dr. Lexton?' Nick demanded, rubbing the back of his head. 'Where does *he* fit into it? Or was he a kind of partner with Royd and the late Uncle Cyrus?'

'I don't think so.' There seemed to be a kind of grim amusement on Len's face. 'Lexton did not appear in this district until after Uncle Cyrus had died. Remember what the police told us?'

'Which seems to make nonsense of Lexton's story that he was a close friend of my Uncle,' Ena reflected. 'Yet, on the other hand, he knew all about that thing in the library so he must have been here quite a lot.'

'I think,' Len said after a long pause, 'that Dr. Lexton and Uncle Cyrus are one and the same person!'

For a moment there was the silence of astonishment; then Nick gave a disbelieving smile.

'You're forgetting a lot of things, Len. Uncle Cyrus was buried. We know he was — so how can he be Lexton?'

'It seems to me,' Len mused, 'that the only way to find out the truth is to question him point blank. I'm sure the theory I've worked out will stand up under fire — '

'How are we to question him when nobody knows where he is?' Ena asked helplessly. 'Even the police cannot find him, so I am certain that we can't!'

'I know the police are looking for him,' Len responded. 'I called in at the police station on my way, just to see how they are getting along. But the police don't know anything about the underground tunnel that leads from the library. The more I think of it the more I believe it may be connected with Lexton's home — a secret route. I suggest we go along it and make sure. That giant ant is probably where it is to prevent anybody moving from one house to the other.'

'Including us,' Nick pointed out grimly. 'You don't suppose we're going to fight that, do you?'

'I do. Because we must.' Len's jaw was taut. 'Lexton is the key to this whole strange business and, if my guess is right, we've got to contact him for his own sake and ours. We might be able to keep that ant at bay with a blazing torch while we get beyond him. There's almost bound to be a continuation of the tunnel beyond the cave, Ena can stay here because of the danger — '

'Ena comes with you,' she interrupted decisively. 'If you two get laid out, then I prefer to be laid out with you. That's the only way I feel safe.'

'Very well then,' Len got to his feet. 'Let's see what we can do,'

So, some ten minutes later, each one of them was armed with an oily piece of wood set alight, with torches in their pockets for emergency, together with a length of strong rope. Thus equipped they entered the tunnel from the library and began to creep along it carefully. It was not long before they turned the corner that gave them a view of the cave at the break in the tunnel. Almost at the same moment they could hear the leathery rustling of the gigantic ant as it stirred at the approach of newcomers.

'Now, we're going to risk everything with this,' Len said, pausing for a moment to get more flame into his torch. 'There is every chance that the tunnel continues beyond the cave so we'll make a dash for it. If it does not then we must detour back to this passageway. It'll be one hell of a risk with a brute like that but I'm convinced we've got to take it.'

Nick and Ena did not argue. To have refused to take the chance would have looked like cowardice, and besides they were as anxious as Len was to get at the truth. So they began following him, brandishing their torches as they went.

The clicking of the giant ant's mandibles became noticeable after a while, then as the three risked everything and burst into the big cavern they saw that frightful monster insect looming not three yards away. It was plain it was fearful of the smoke and flames from the torches.

'Run for it!' Len cried. 'It's our only chance.'

At top speed he raced across the cavern towards its opposite wall, and at the same time the giant ant hurled towards him. Instantly Nick threw his torch. It struck the insect on the head and it wheeled around, bristling. The monstrous compound eyes glared with satanic fury, then the terrible mouth of the thing lashed and snapped outwards. Nick hurtled to one side, dragging Ena after him. She caught her foot in the rough flooring and stumbled — and instantly the ant was upon her.

Before it could drive its pincer-like appendages into her slim body, however, Len had come on the scene. Using his own torch he battered it savagely across the insect's face and aimed the flames at

76

the enormous hypnotic eyes. Frightened for the moment the thing withdrew. In that time Nick was able to snatch Ena up from the floor and hold her to him as he kept on running.

Len's guess that the tunnel would continue beyond the cave was correct. Nick and Ena came upon it suddenly and floundered into it. Only a few seconds after them came Len. A frightful pincer arm lashed out at him as he hurtled into the dark vista and by inches he escaped. Then the baffled termite was held at bay by reason of the tunnel's narrowness. Its mandibles clicked in fury and it made frantic efforts to wedge itself into the small space.

'Apparently it's fighting mad,' Len said. 'We'd better get going in case it finds a way to squeeze after us.'

He whipped out his electric torch and, fanning the beam in front of him, raced up the narrow vista. It went on and on, turning corners occasionally, until at last it ended in a metal door.

'Now what?' Nick asked breathlessly, the torch beam playing on the door rivets.

'Nothing short of dynamite would break down a door like this — '

He stopped speaking, his mouth open in surprise as the door began to swing inwards silently, as if moved by hidden springs. When it came to a stop it was wide open, giving a view of a quietly lighted surgery beyond. There did not appear to be anybody about.

'This explains much,' Len said, moving forward slowly. 'This is probably where the ant experiments were made. Remember, we couldn't find a laboratory or surgery anywhere? Here it is. As for the door, it must be made to open if anybody comes along the passage — photo-electric cell principle probably. Since nobody was likely to come with that brute in the way the door was not locked. Maybe it won't lock at all except by selenium cell reaction. Anyway, we're learning things.'

He kept on moving as he talked, Nick and Ena immediately behind him. They looked about them as they went. There seemed to be every type of surgical necessity. The lighting was indirect, flooding down from a cream-painted ceiling at the edges of which were concealed lamps.

The trio made no effort to touch anything. They had only one absorbing quest — to find Dr. Lexton. And, quite unexpectedly they did, in the room that was continuous to the surgery. It had no door — only an opening in the wall — so that they came upon it suddenly.

They stopped dead, thunderstruck,

Dr. Lexton was seated in a low-built chair in the centre of a small room, his back to the three standing petrified in the doorway. The nauseating thing about the room was that it literally crawled with ants. They were thick on the walls, hardly moving, and clustered around gigantic bowls fixed in alcoves in the walls. From these bowls there stretched slack tubes which ended in one mouthpiece, rather like a hookah. Lexton had the mouth-piece between his lips. Now and again one of his hands reached out lazily and whisked a feather duster round the ants in the globes.

'What the devil's going on?' Nick whispered huskily.

Len watched the amazing performance intently, then he answered.

'Those insects clustered round the bowls are what are called stomach-ants. They are living baskets. They absorb honeydew and regurgitate it when their stomachs are lightly dusted with a feather.'

'Looks horrible to me,' Ena said in disgust. 'Do you actually mean that Lexton is drinking, or sucking honeydew from the horrible things?'

'Yes, I — '

Suddenly Lexton was on his feet — a strange, terrifying little figure. Unwittingly Len had raised his voice in answering Ena and now — Lexton no longer looked like the suave doctor with the hypnotic voice. He was a weird being with two terrible eyes that had no spectacles to render them obscure. They seemed to be huge hypnotic pupils with no whites or irises. There was a distinct mental shock from him as he stood staring. Then his hand closed round an automatic on the table beside him. He levelled it steadily.

'And what is the meaning of this?' he asked, forcing himself to be deliberate and, in a remote sort of way, even courteous.

Len took up the conversation in the same strain.

'The intrusion was not intentional, Dr. Lexton. We came upon you unexpectedly . . . Or *is* it Dr. Lexton? Would I not be more correct in saying Cyrus Odder, the only man on this planet who ever became an ant?'

'Ant?' Ena repeated, dazed. '*Him?*'

'That's my guess,' Len said deliberately, still looking at the motionless little gnome of a man. 'I believe that you are Cyrus Odder and that with Dr. Royd you made unbelievable progress into entomological science. I further believe that your insatiable desire for insect knowledge led you to have your brain transferred into the body of a giant ant — which makes you half human and half ant, your body really being that of an ant cleverly disguised. The Cyrus Odder who was buried intact — except for his

81

brain, and what doctor giving a certificate would ever think of looking to see if the corpse's brain was there?'

'I think,' Lexton said, putting the automatic in his pocket and then perching his minimising spectacles on his beaked nose, 'that we would be more comfortable discussing in the surgery. This termitarium is hardly a place which can appeal to you.'

He led the way to the surgery, pausing when he had reached chairs near one of the operating tables. He motioned to them, but he himself remained standing, his hand in his pocket and obviously gripping the automatic.

'Yes,' he admitted quietly, 'I am Cyrus Odder — or at least my brain is. The rest of me is in the ground.'

'Uncle, what have you done?' Ena demanded huskily, 'Whatever made you perform such diabolical experiments?'

'Diabolical?' He laughed shortly. 'Ena, my child, you always were a thoughtless little fool. As a young girl you were a nuisance, and now as a grown woman you are empty headed. You dare to call this

82

mighty experiment with the termite world diabolical?'

'I think she's correct,' Nick said bluntly. 'By what right do you meddle with Creation and change your genus entirely? What's the object?'

'Hear my story,' Odder commanded, 'With the help of Dr. Royd, a brilliant brain surgeon and also interested in termites, I created a hybrid ant — yet in all senses it was a true specimen — '

'I know,' Len interrupted. 'I've been checking back on the unfortunate Dr. Royd.'

'I see; then that saves a lot of needless explanation. We provided it with synthetic lungs and it grew with staggering speed, evolving a true size and might for the first time. We had to keep it in captivity, so we put it in the cave between the two tunnels connecting this laboratory and house with my former home. And, of course, we kept it fed.'

'You mean you owned this house even when you were Odder?' Nick asked.

'I did, yes, but not under my own name. I used it for many scientific experiments, but most of the experiments took place in my surgery here or one or other of the various underground rooms I had made. I kept the house furnished and invented a mythical owner who had gone abroad, from whom I apparently bought the property when I became Lexton. I knew I was going to become Lexton one day. When that happened I had to assume the new personality so as to convince everybody I was not Cyrus Odder, dead and buried. Apparently you, Mr. Chalmers, have been remarkably sagacious.'

'I suspected you were an ant-man the moment I first saw you,' Len answered. 'From then on I set out to prove it.'

'Mmmm — clever of you,' Odder sneered. 'Anyhow, the issue of my becoming Lexton was taken out of my hands and I was *compelled* to. Too late, Royd and I realized that we had created a true ant in *every* way. It possessed a diabolically powerful intelligence, far stronger than ours with its fifty-million-year old heritage. Though trapped in the cave down there its mental force was sufficient to reach me; whether I was here or in my own home. Consider for a moment that even the normal ant is ruled by a central intelligence which has utter domination over thousands of slave ants; then multiply the effect a thousand-fold for the giant ant and you can see how much power the thing in the cellar has.'

Cyrus Odder was silent for a moment, then as he continued his tone assumed a hopeless quality.

'This fiendish thing, which knows no pity to a human being or to anything outside its own race, commanded of me that I become the intermediary between the ant and the human world. I could not disobey. Under orders, Royd and I enlarged a neuter ant to human size by the same process as we had created our dreaded hybrid, and after that Royd was forced by mental compulsion to put my brain into the body of that ant. When that was done I was half-ant and half-human, with artificial vocal chords — which accounts for my unusual voice, by the way.'

'Then?' Nick prompted, as Odder relapsed into speculation.

'When the operation was complete Royd had to obey the ruling of the ant and dispose of my body. Accordingly it was done in quite a natural way. It was dumped outside my home and left there, the assumption being that I had died of heart failure. I had overlooked, however, that in my pocket I carried a letter to be opened in the event of my death. I had a bad heart, of course, so in that respect I cannot say I regret losing that other body — but that letter brought you into the 'Cedars,' Ena — the one thing I did not want but was powerless to prevent.'

'Which was why you tried to buy us out?' Nick asked.

'Yes — and it cost me great effort of will, too. The great ant commanded that I destroy all three of you. I, on the other hand, fought that command and tried to make you leave. I failed. The ant's mental compulsion killed your father, Ena, or perhaps you had guessed that?'

'So it was the ant,' Ena breathed, clenching her fists.

'I sensed it — somehow. It came so

soon after Dad had been having queer delusions . . . '

'Mental probings,' Odder explained. 'The ant was feeling its strength. It seeks nothing less than the destruction of all things human and the absolute domination of its own race. The ferocious hatred of the ant for the human cannot even be imagined unless you are, as I am, in tune with the ant-mind. Just as I was forced to kill Dr. Royd in case he told too much. I thought him safely out of the way until you started to investigate: then I tried to move him and made things worse than ever. Since then I have been a prisoner down here, feeding — as an ant does — on honeydew. Up above the police are waiting to arrest me. I would willingly let them only I feel it is my duty to stay here. As long as I am alive I am able to some extent to subdue the giant ant my perverted genius created. If I died it would be free to do as it wishes — with the most appalling consequences.'

'I had already foreseen that,' Len commented. 'But one ant of itself cannot cause any damage. The police have only to be informed and they'll kill it instantly.'

'Kill it?' Odder repeated, aghast. 'Kill it? Wipe out my beautiful creation with their guns and explosives? No, Mr. Chalmers. Though I am under the domination of my own creations I have an affection for it. It represents the product of a vast stride forward in entomological science. As long as it is locked by its own size in that cave it can do no harm — no real harm — though it can mesmerise me. It will also try and destroy you three later unless you get out of its range as I have begged you to do. It probably finds you all difficult to break down, however. You are young and vital and have tremendous resistance. Such a case did not apply with your father, Ena.'

'The fact remains,' Nick said, 'that ghastly thing has got to be destroyed — and it shall be. As for you, there is only one rightful place for you — an asylum! Sorry to be so blunt, but you're a public menace with this ant ruling your movements.'

'Do you realize what would happen if this giant ant forced you to create a female with which it could mate?' Len asked curtly.

'I do. Before long a race of giant ants would spawn and humanity would not be worth a jot. That is why I keep the female locked up behind steel doors.'

There was a momentary startled pause. Lexton — Odder — looked from one to the other.

'You mean you have made a female?' Nick gasped at last.

'Yes, indeed. I was compelled to do so — but I fought the compulsion far enough to keep the female away from the male. She has not the same mental dominance as the other insect so I am not swayed by her thoughts. If you disbelieve me, look here . . . '

Odder moved across the surgery to a massive steel door inset into the wall. He drew back the heavy bolts and swung the door wide. The three looked intently into the shadowy gloom beyond, then out of it there began to emerge an object every whit as terrifying as the creature in the cave, only perhaps not so big. Otherwise it was identical. The stalked eyes, the vast hairy legs, the mandibles and pincer forelegs.

It was a sudden sound to the rear which made Ena wheel round. Her face went pale and she gripped Nick's arm. He gave a hoarse gasp. Emerging out of the tunnel beyond the surgery, squeezing itself with stupendous effort, was the insect from the cave, its terrifying eyes glaring in malignant fury. Somehow it had succeeded in forcing its huge body along, probably spurred on by the desire for vengeance on the humans who had thrown flaming torches into its face.

'Run for it!' Len cried in alarm, looking desperately about him. 'Mr. Odder, shut that steel door — ! If these two insects meet each other — '

But Odder was in no fit state to do anything. Utterly mesmerised by the eyes of the creature that was his master he could only stand staring at it, held by mental compulsion. And since the giant ant could not concentrate on more than one person at a time Len seized his chance and whipped up a heavy instrument case. But before he could hurl it at the thing just dragging itself through the doorway into the surgery the female darted from her prison and landed a smashing blow with one foreleg. It caught Len across the back of the head and sent him spinning against the wall, the instrument case dropping out of his grip.

Immediately Nick and Ena chased after him. They dragged him up and went floundering into the termitarium beyond. Then realizing it had no openings — any more than the upper part of the house had chimneys — they reeled out again and hurried to the far end of the surgery. As they went they saw Odder for the last time, going down helplessly before the rending mandibles and pincer claws of the two giant termites he had created. All his wish to be an intermediary had ended in his death. His long drawn out fight against the compulsion of the master-ant was over. It was concerned now only with the fact that it had found another of its own species, and of the opposite sex.

This preoccupation at least gave Nick,

Ena, and Len the one chance they needed to escape. They watched their opportunity and, at a convenient moment, fled down the narrow tunnel up which they had come, assured that the ants could not follow them at any speed. Gasping and dishevelled they raced through the big cave and then beyond it into the tunnel's continuation. It seemed unbelievable to them, when they came into the library in the sunlight of the autumn afternoon that everything could be so quiet, so ordinary, so everyday.

'We'll have to fix this door,' Len said curtly, slamming over the slide. 'Best thing we can do is weld it into position. Maybe I could borrow a welding apparatus from the garage in the village.'

'Maybe,' Nick agreed, too preoccupied with horrible memories to think straight. 'Len, what happens now?'

'Everything.' His eyes were bleak. 'That is unless we act quickly. We must inform the police what has happened and try and get them to destroy these two monsters before any more harm can be done. We'd better all go to the village immediately and see what we can do. Come on.'

Just for a moment Ena remembered in the confusion that her father's dead body was lying upstairs, waiting for burial on the morrow. She had a vision of one, or both, ants emerging into this library, finding the corpse, and then desecrating it. If they did — Well, it would be ghastly, harrowing, but there was nothing she could do about it. It was the living who were in danger now, not the dead.

She raced after Nick and Len from the house and to the car, still standing in the front as Len had left it on his return from London. In another moment Nick had the car moving fast, speeding down the dreary drive and out into the lane.

He had hardly covered two hundred yards before Ena, sitting beside him, gripped his arm so tightly he nearly lost his hold on the steering wheel. He glanced at her in alarm.

'What on earth are you trying to do?' he demanded irritably. 'I nearly over-turned there — '

'Stop!' Ena insisted, looking at some-thing in the distance through the side window. 'What's going on over there — at Uncle's house?'

'Going on?' Nick looked bewildered.

'Hell, yes!' Len exclaimed, startled. 'Stop — quickly!'

The brakes shrieked and the car tyres bit into the gravel. Nick swung round in his seat — then he saw what Ena and Len had meant. From this position the house on the hill was clearly visible, and outside it something incredible — and in fact alarming — was going on. A police constable, dimly visible as a tiny figure with the slanting sunlight reflecting from the silvered top of his helmet, was running for his life. Behind him loomed two gigantic insects, moving at a far greater speed than he was. The outcome was inevitable. Suddenly he stumbled and fell.

Ena swung her head away, her lips tight. Nick and Len continued looking. At their distance from the incident they could not discern the details, but imagination supplied them.

'Somehow,' Nick said at last, 'those infernal ants must have got out of the underground. And I can't think how.'

'I can,' Len snapped. 'There must be more ways into that underground surgery and termitarium of Odder's than the tunnel we found. He had that made as an extra — a communication from house to house. Naturally he must have had a way from his own house into the underground, and those ants found it, either by accident or design. It's all up with that poor devil of a constable, anyway ... That's bad enough, but the tough part is that those infernal ants are free and running wild. If they mate and produce others — as they certainly will — almost anything can happen!'

'They're on the move again,' Ena said, turning her gaze back to the window. 'How do you suppose they can ever be caught now?'

'They've got to be, somehow,' Len answered tautly. 'Keep going, Nick, to the police station. Never mind that welding apparatus: it's obviously too late now.'

'And the policeman?' Nick asked. 'Don't we give him some help?'

'He'll be beyond it, or I don't know

giant termites. It is those who are still alive who need protection — Step on it, man, there's no time to lose.'

Nick started the engine up again and then gave the car all it had got on its journey to the village. The local inspector was in his office and looked up expectantly from his desk as, after the sergeant had, announced them, the three came into his sanctum.

'Glad to see you again, Mrs. Hansley, Mr. — '

'No time for formalities,' Len interrupted, almost rudely. 'Inspector, get every man you can and arm him — and inform the nearest army headquarters. Two giant ants are abroad in the countryside and unless they are wiped out they will prove a bigger menace than all the armies of a human invader.'

'Ants? Armies? What the devil are you talking about?'

It seemed incredible to the three that the inspector had not the remotest idea of what was transpiring — but of course he had not. So he had to be told in detail, and as the story unfolded his bushy eyebrows went higher and his mouth opened wider.

'Dr. Lexton was Cyrus Odder?' he repeated at last, sitting down with a thump in his swivel chair. 'His brain transferred into the body of an enlarged neuter ant? Now look here, Mr. Chalmers — '

'For heavens' sake get a move on!' Len insisted. 'With every passing minute those ants will become more difficult to locate. Don't you *understand?*'

'No, I do not!' the inspector retorted. 'What do you take me for? I never heard such damned fantastic nonsense in all my life! I'm not sure I oughtn't to run the three of you in for playing tricks with the law — '

'If that's how you feel about it go and take a look at your constable who was guarding the Lexton house!' Nick snapped.

'All right, I'll do that much,' the inspector conceded ill-humouredly, 'But I'll reserve my judgment as to whether he was killed by so-called giant ants — or not.'

'Meaning what?' Len demanded.

'Meaning that there's a lot of queer

things going on in this district at present.' The inspector got to his feet with menace in his eyes. 'So far, Mr. Chalmers, I've taken you at your word that you *found* the body of Dr. Royd and *saw* Dr. Lexton near it — but I haven't been able to prove it, have I? I've not been able to get hold of Lexton, and now you say he is dead. Not only that, but he isn't Lexton at all but Cyrus Odder, whom we know is buried in south-east London.'

'Without his brain,' Nick put in curtly.

'Maybe.' There was sour disbelief in the inspector's expression. 'Anyway, I'll take a look around and then form my own judgment.'

He summoned his sergeant and gave him brief directions. In a little while the police car was following Nick's car up the lane. Nick was fuming silently and Ena was tight-lipped. Len was looking grim.

'Our own fault,' he said bitterly. 'We should have gone straight to the authorities in Clancester. This country nitwit is going to be more of a hindrance than a help . . . It isn't the body of the constable that matters so much anyway. It's the fact that those two ants are loose.'

Since there was nothing to be gained by talking Nick remained silent, and so did Ena. Presently they reached the point of the lane nearest to the position where they had seen the constable attacked. Nick drew to a halt and climbed out of the car to meet the inspector and sergeant as they came forward.

'Up the bank here,' Nick said, and led the way.

It was ten minutes later when, in the lengthening evening sunlight beams they came upon the constable's body. Ena only glanced at it and even then she felt momentarily faint. No such disability touched the inspector. He eyed the mangled body, nearly ripped limb from limb and then looked coldly at Nick and Len,

'And I'm supposed to believe that ants did this?' he demanded.

'Giant ones,' Nick corrected, his voice grim.

'Mmmm.' The inspector glanced at the sergeant. 'Send for the boys to come and take this body away,' he ordered. 'I'm going to look a bit further — '

'Over there!' Len shouted suddenly, grabbing the inspector's arm and pointing. 'Now do you believe it?'

The inspector stared, blankly, but even he could not discredit the evidence of his own eyes. Perhaps half a mile away clearly visible against the western sunlight, two vast insectile outlines were visible. They had reared up for a moment or two and appeared to be surveying; then they got on the move again.

'Hell!' the inspector said, his face suddenly greasy. 'No doubt about that . . . ' He swung. 'I'm sorry, Mr. Chalmers. I owe you an apology. I never saw insects that big before.'

'Apologies don't signify; it's action we want,' Len responded. 'We've got to capture those two brutes somehow and kill them. I suppose you don't carry a gun?'

'No. I'm afraid not.' The inspector was looking towards the spot where the insects were now dimly visible against the dark background of the countryside. He asked a question, 'Suppose there's nothing we can do without firearms? While they're in sight, I mean.'

'Nothing.' Len was quite decisive. 'You saw what they did to the constable: they would do the same to us. Apart from that, the bigger one — the male — has powerful brain force. It could hypnotise us if we got within range.'

'Insects with hypnotic power?' The inspector was obviously bewildered, but he had at least learned not to doubt Len Chalmer's word. 'Then what *do* we do?'

'Only one thing we *can* do,' Len decided, after a pause. 'You must notify all police stations and military authorities to be on the alert for these insects and to kill them on sight. They will do that if you ask them, since you are an officer of the law. Also, everybody around this district must be warned, by house-to-house warning if need be, to stay indoors until these monsters have been wiped out. The danger is real, Inspector, and deadly. But if we act now we ought to be able to take care of it. The trouble will come if these ants mate and leave eggs behind. Since like species promote like offspring the progeny will also be giants. You understand?'

'Uh-huh,' the inspector muttered. 'I understand — and I'd better get busy right away.'

# 5

## Insect attack

The inspector wasted no time, and whereas he had formerly been a 'Doubting Thomas' he was now entirely on the side of Len Chalmers. He managed to convince an irate head of the military division and argued his point with the authorities in Clancester. Clancester sent a fleet of walkie-talkie cars and they patrolled up and down the inhabited byways issuing warnings to a decidedly puzzled populace.

By nightfall the situation was somewhat in hand, though nothing definite had been achieved. Truckloads of grinning soldiers armed with rifles and automatic weapons were driven to various points of concealment and afterwards deployed over the night-ridden landscape in search of the monsters. By midnight a dragnet twelve miles in extent was in operation.

Len did not let the matter stop here. From the village he telephoned the President of the Entomology Institution in London and gave him the details, chiefly because he felt he might need the backing of that august and learned gentleman at a later date if the ant menace grew to sizeable proportions. This done, he felt he had made every move possible in so far as protecting the population was concerned — so he returned to The Cedars to rejoin Nick and Ena and await events.

The police took charge of Odder-cum-Lexton's home on the hill, discovered how the ants had broken out from below through a panelling in the hall and then through a window, and also had the battered corpse in the underground laboratory removed for surgical examination. The various papers that were found in the house were quite sufficient to prove that Odder had spoken the truth — and it was further verified when, that same night, his body in south-east London was exhumed by permission of the Home Secretary and found to be without a brain.

It was towards midnight when the inspector himself called at The Cedars to give this information. He had three very grave — and, as far as Len was concerned, very tired — people to listen to him.

'So what happens now is entirely up to the militia,' he finished. 'I thought you would want to know what is going on. I misjudged you so much at first you are entitled to know everything.'

'There are some things I don't know,' Len said, slumped deep in an armchair. 'Maybe you found the answers in the various records kept by Odder. Did he say exactly how he got a horde of ants to wipe out a bed of nettles?'

'Er — yes. I seem to remember seeing such a statement . . . ' The inspector looked through his notes. 'Yes, here it is! He said — I quote — 'I think I have convinced my niece, her husband, and a friend by the name of Chalmers, that it would be best for them to leave. Last night, to my niece and her husband, I gave a demonstration of the power of a superior ant-human mind over that of neuter ants. I made them destroy a bed of nettles. It was simple, since all neuters obey a stronger central intelligence. The ground, of course, teems with neuter ants, invisible to the passer-by who has his mind on other things, so it was not difficult to bring them to action!' That ends the statement.'

'Interesting,' Len commented. 'Does he refer to the absence of chimneys in his house?'

'Yes, but I haven't the actual notes. I understand he had all chimneys removed to prevent unnecessary draught. That house-cum-termitarium of his was like a hothouse, the only way, I gathered, to keep it at a fit temperature for his little playmates. I think,' the inspector finished, 'that Dr. Lexton — or rather Cyrus Odder — fought a mighty hard battle not only with the ants he created, but with himself. On the one hand he wanted the domination he might achieve by being an ant-man; yet on the other he tried to prevent the real ant from getting the better of him.

Between the two he lost his life.'

'And the worst,' Len mused, 'has probably yet to come.'

'I sincerely hope not, sir.' The inspector had risen, full of the importance of his position. 'We'll get the matter under control, Mr. Chalmers — never fear.'

Len only smiled and rose to shake hands. When the inspector had gone the trio looked at one another.

'All we can do now,' Nick said, spreading his hands, 'is to try and live normally until we hear what happens. No reason why the army and the police working in concert shouldn't locate those ants — and the airforce is spying out the land as well, remember. By morning I don't doubt we will hear of success.'

And, though he doubted his own statement, he proved to be correct. He was at breakfast with Ena and Len when the inspector made an early call.

'Good news, sir,' the inspector exclaimed genially as Nick opened the door to him. 'We got both those brutes in the early hours. They were in the fields three miles from Clanchester. We blew 'em to pieces!

Or at least the militia did. A few grenades settled the matter.'

The inspector had come into the big breakfast room at the close of his statement and he looked in surprise as Len Chalmers aimed a question at him.

'You mean to say those bone-headed soldiers actually blew those ants to bits?'

'Definitely!' The inspector was looking supremely pleased with himself. 'After all, you did say they ought to be destroyed, sir.'

'I know I did, but I didn't mean so thoroughly. You have cheated science of two of the finest specimen the world has ever known! I don't know what the President of the Entomology Institution is going to say!'

'Frankly, Mr. Chalmers, that doesn't concern me in the least. We'd been ordered to destroy a danger, and we've done it. Everybody can rest easy now — and if you ever feel like writing a book on the subject you've some good material.'

Len did not respond. He sat down again at the table and continued with his breakfast. The inspector, his message of good cheer delivered, took his departure.

'Which would seem to put everything on an even keel,' Nick commented. 'We have only your father's funeral to deal with, Ena, and then maybe we can straighten out our lives somewhat. As for you, Len — what do you propose doing?'

Len shrugged. 'Return to London and forget all about this business. Naturally I'm glad it's over, but I had hoped secretly for something exciting. Still, there it is.'

As he had said, there it was — and immediately after the funeral of Ena's father, who was buried at the cemetery just beyond the nearby village, Len returned to London. For Nick and Ena there was just the future in the 'Cedars,' and plans to bring it more up to date. So, as the weeks of autumn passed by and winter spread its iron grip across the country they gradually forgot the advent of the giant ants and Uncle Cyrus's astounding experiment.

Len Chalmers, however, always a scientist at heart, spent much of his spare time at the 'Cedars,' indulging in long walks at intervals, yet never explaining them as anything else but exercise. Until he discovered something important. It was just before Easter when this happened — a particularly warm spring — and he had come up for the Easter holiday. His first day's walk into the surrounding country had brought him back to the house full of excitement.

'I believe I'm right!' he declared, without explaining himself. 'Come and see what I've discovered.'

'Er — do we need a car?' Nick asked, glancing at Ena in surprise.

'No — no, we can walk it. Only about, a mile across the fields, not far from your Uncle's former abode, Ena.'

She glanced towards it through the big window. It had become nothing more than a sightseer's curiosity these days since, naturally, the story of the ants and their creator had — at the time — been given to a surprised world, It was as she glanced that she saw something else, and frowned,

'I never noticed that weird looking hill

before!' she exclaimed in surprise. 'See it? To the right of the rise where the house is standing.'

'That's what I want you to look at,' Len said urgently. 'Let's be on our way.'

His urgency did not permit of delay so Ena and Nick followed him from the house and across the fields. There was the warmth of an early summer in the air. The sky was blue, the clouds serene, the fields brilliant with the yellow of butter-cups and dandelions. And ahead was this strange looking hill, all of forty or fifty feet in height and perhaps close on a mile wide. In appearance it looked remarkably like a sugar-loaf.

'What the devil is it?' Nick demanded, when they had actually reached it.

Len prodded it with the stick he was carrying. The hill was as hard as iron. From inside it, in response to the blows he gave, there came a mysterious rising and falling note like bees suddenly disturbed.

'As I thought,' he said, his face becoming grim. 'Full of life. In case you don't know it, this thing is a gigantic termitarium. Note the size of it! An ordinary one is sometimes fifteen feet high, when it houses normal ants. Since this one is so gigantic it obviously houses *giant* ants.'

'What!' Ena gasped, horrified. 'Are you bringing up *that* horrible business again, Len?'

'Believe me, I don't want to. But I've been afraid of this happening for long enough. That is why I have been prowling about for so long, looking for signs of ant life left behind from those ants which were blown to pieces last autumn.'

'But — but didn't that end things?' Nick looked bewildered.

'Far from it! I think it only started then. Don't forget those two ants which escaped had plenty of time to mate and the female can lay eggs at prodigious speed when necessary. That, I think, is what happened — but they didn't hatch until the warm weather came. Here we see the result. In here,' — Len banged the termitarium again with his stick — 'I'll gamble there are thousands of giant ants of every type and breed — neuters, soldiers, kings, and queens, each in their own social scale. When they emerge, as I believe they will when they have things organized, we'll have the biggest battle ever on our hands. I must get in touch with the authorities right away and have everywhere searched for other termitaria. They must be wiped out before anything happens.'

He swung round and began hurrying back towards the distant 'Cedars.' Ena and Nick gave another look at the termitarium, then they turned and followed him, more disturbed in mind than they had been since the fateful night when the male and female red ants had escaped from Cyrus Odder's laboratory.

In an hour Len had communicated his information to all those men whom he believed would deal promptly with the matter, and once again the world began to buzz to rumours of possible invasion by insect-life. Starting the next day the little village near Clancester became the focus of a world spotlight as scientists, entomologists, commanders of the militia, and police officials all converged to

113

study the termitarium ... Then the airforce reported that other termitaria were also present in other parts of the country — and in Europe, too — so attention became more general than particular.

Nobody made any attempt to break into the termitaria and examine them. This would have been far too risky. Instead they were bombed by aircraft until they no longer existed. To a certain extent this seemed to smash the danger — until more termitaria bobbed up in various directions, created by the busy beings within them, until by the time the hot summer was well advanced it took one section of the airforce all its time to keep on destroying the queer creations.

To Len, when he had time to think about the matter apart from his normal work, it seemed more than strange that no insects ever emerged to do battle. There were never any reports of any giant neuroptera being seen. Satisfactory though this was to the military and air force brass hats preening themselves at

114

their success in keeping down the menace, it was anything but it to the scientists and entomologists studying the problem. To this august little body of experts Len had become admitted, chiefly in respect for his lone efforts to tackle the problem.

Towards mid-summer, at one of the meetings in the Entomology Institution in London, his views were asked for — and he gave them, the famous entomologists around the table listening to him attentively.

'I confess to being deeply worried, gentlemen,' he said. 'An ant that does not actively engage in some task or other just is not to be thought of. If it is not visible on the surface doing something, then it must be doing a tremendous lot below. What? That is what I would give anything to know. I do not have to tell you gentlemen here how intelligent is even a normal ant, how it has the gift of organization and can plan everything with the sagacity of a military commander. The giant species, such as must rule in these termitaria, will *also* be able to plan — and that is what I am afraid of. That they are hatching some gigantic scheme which will overthrow us humans when it materializes.'

'Overthrow us, Mr. Chalmers?' The President of the Institute gave an indulgent smile. 'Surely that is a little fanciful?'

'On the contrary, sir. Remember that I encountered the original giant ant and I know how terrible an insect it was. It possessed hypnotic power as well as organizing genius. It was infinitely cleverer than any human because it was backed by the fifty million years of inheritance every ant possesses. For a long time now I have been expecting some kind of hypnosis to descend on the human race, produced by the insects below — but it has not happened. It is this perfect peace that bothers me. Something is *brewing*! And to just bomb the termitaria does no good at all. Fresh ones appear constantly.'

'You think we should cease our bombardment, then?' one of the delegates asked.

'Since it is a waste of manpower and materials, yes. Instead I think we — and every country in the world — should look to our armaments against the day when the termites do strike. For they will eventually — and with such brilliant organization that we may well be wiped out. Remember the ants will show us no mercy. They are the rightful inheritors of Earth. We of the human race are only here because Nature made us more adaptable than the ant. That day has gone. There are two races on Earth now, manoeuvring — I believe — for position.'

Len had little more than this to say, but a vote upon his motion to cease bombarding the termitaria was carried, as was his notion to tighten up defence strategy against — What? No commander knew. No man knew. What would it be like to fight not human beings but mighty insects backed by an intelligence which had, thanks to Cyrus Odder's dabblings, reached a staggering peak? Fantastic! Impossible! Perhaps —

And still nothing happened, and the strain on the nerves of humanity was intense. The termitaria, unhindered now, sprouted in all parts of the world — and it was the very fact that they were present equally in Britain or Australia, Russia or China, that gave Len cause for more worry, It looked as if the ants below had the whole planet at their mercy and could move anywhere independent of distance.

Nick and Ena still living at The Cedars went on with their daily lives because there was nothing else they could do — but around their home, at a distance of perhaps a mile, there were clustered no less than nine gigantic termitaria. At any time they might release hordes of giant termites. On the other hand, no part of the country was any safer, so they remained where they were. Nick even became accustomed, in driving to London and back daily, to passing between the giant hills of iron-hard earth that the busy insects had created.

Then, towards the close of the furiously hot summer, there came new signs and wonders, and it was the Reverend Horace Hancock who was one of the first to encounter them. He was the local preacher for the tiny village of Greater Carpington in Surrey and, as is common with such gentlemen in the summer, he had arranged a Sunday outing for the parents and children of his flock. It had been decided that a picnic should take place in Layton's Field, due permission having been obtained from the farmer-owner.

The day was all a summer day should be — nearly ninety in the shade with the sun a molten ball of brass in cobalt heavens. A day for butterflies, birds, and every creeping thing to take advantage. The smiling vicar in his french grey, surrounded by men and women of his parish, together with the romping children, was at peace with the world. He selected a giant tree for shade and under it the laughing party, loaded with baskets, began to disport.

Then came a buzzing. The Reverend Horace looked at the sky, expecting to behold an airplane on a practice flight. Instead he received the shock of his blameless life. Sweeping out of the cloudless heaven there came quite the biggest bee — or wasp — or something, which he had ever seen. It had a wingspan from tip to tip of something like fifty feet, and its body was all of a hundred. In some peculiar way it *was* a bee, yet in another it was quite different. A kind of hybrid species with the strain of a hornet and something else added.

The reverend gentleman had no time to notice these details at that moment; they returned as later memories. He was too busy flinging himself flat as with a noise like a small jet plane the monster shot past overhead. Instantly panic burst amidst the picnickers. They began to run, stumbling over the baskets, catching their feet in the basins, tripping in the half laid tablecloths.

Running as they did from the protection of the big tree was the very last thing they should have done, and the vicar knew it. Even as he scrambled to his feet, shouting hoarsely for his flock to return, the bee-wasp-something swung round in a tremendous arc and came zipping back. As it moved it released a frightful barbed sting from its rear. It struck stout Mrs.

Barton clean in the back and slammed her on to her face . . . Nor did she move again.

The vicar called on heaven and man to help him, and then realized he was perhaps the only man worth mentioning. The other men had fled and the women were bundling their children along away from the flying horror. The Rev. Horace Hancock was the only one who did not run. He had faith in his conviction that the Lord is the right hand of man — so he picked up the long prop on which the basket had been carried from the shoulders of the campers, held it like an athlete about to perform a pole-vault, and waited for the monster to come back.

It did — at dizzying speed, and at that moment the Reverend Horace translated into action the story of David and Goliath. He slammed the pole point first straight into the striped belly of the monster as it zipped overhead at only ten feet height. It gave a vast piping scream and, for a moment, still flew on with the pole jutting from its body. Then it faltered, and finally crashed to earth some twenty feet away. For quite a time it lay fluttering like a butterfly transfixed by a nasty small boy's pin — until at last the struggling ceased.

The Reverend Horace wiped the perspiration from his face and, advanced slowly. He discovered that the monster was quite dead, its huge faceted eyes glazing, a pale humour pouring from its immense and yet beautiful body where the pole had impaled it. By some fluke the Reverend Horace had struck a vital spot.

He was quivering with the reaction. He turned and realized the campers were coming towards him, some shame-faced, others too bewildered to speak. A little girl's voice piped up.

'What is it, vicar? A big wasp?'

'The biggest the world has ever seen, my dear,' he answered, his voice shaky. 'I am sure the Good Lord knows what He is about, but I do think He was over-generous on this occasion. I — I think we should return home. Per — perhaps this place is not altogether suitable for a picnic . . . '

And in under an hour the Reverend Horace Hancock's name was being sent across the world by every means of communication. He was a hero, a true man of God, a perfect example of a protector — and many other things. At the risk of own life he had slain a monster bee-wasp-something

The scientists got on the move. A bee-wasp-something with a body a hundred feet long was worth looking at and an erudite deputation travelled immediately to Greater Carpington, With them was Len Chalmers and, at his request, Nick and Ena had joined him. In the soft light of the summer evening the party stood looking at the dead insect with the pole still projecting from its magnificent body.

'Without doubt a hornet with strains of the bee — and the ant,' Len said finally, and the wiseheads around him nodded somberly.

'But how does such a thing come about?' Ena asked, puzzled.

'It is an example of cross-breeding performed by the giant ants,' Len answered seriously. 'Obviously the eggs of a queen bee have been fertilized somehow by male ants of the giant species, which, as is natural to biology, has produced strains of both the ant and the bee — the giantism of the one and the appearance of the other. That, I think, is the basis — but here we have a distinct strain of the hornet well, which seems to suggest the eggs of an ant, or a bee, cross-fertilised again by a hornet, producing a three-in-one variation of highly dangerous characteristics. When one considers that a queen bee, for instance, lays about eighteen thousand eggs, we realize the enormity of our problem. There may be tens of thousands of gigantic bees, wasps, hornets and, other insects hidden somewhere below ground. The giant ants obviously have undisputed mastery of the insect world and will bend every other insect to their will and purpose. What happened in this case I don't know. Maybe this one escaped somehow.'

'And attacked human beings instantly,' Nick pointed out. 'That's the part I don't like. Do you suppose the giant ants, our mortal enemies, can somehow infuse other insects with their own sense of merciless hatred?'

'Quite possible,' Len admitted, sighing, 'when we consider the tremendous mental power they possess . . . I am very much afraid this thing here is just one out of a titanic armada of flying horrors which may one day be released upon us, much as an invading nation sends its air force to soften up resistance before advancing. A normal ant would be up to a trick like that. As for a super one — !'

He did not say any more. The future was too dire with possibilities for him to need to enlarge upon it. With the scientists he returned to London, and Nick and Ena went back to The Cedars — Then everybody waited for what might happen next.

And on the never-to-be-forgotten morning of August 28th the long threatening storm broke.

Towards dawn on that morning, following a hot and thundery night, there came throughout the daylit side of the world a deep droning, like the advance of tens of thousands of heavy aircraft. At this hour most people were asleep or else in restless slumber because of the stifling weather — but there were also many hundreds who were not. Those at the defence posts, out at sea, in lonely watch-towers, and they first caught the sounds and wondered what was happening. The fantastic idea of invasion by insects was still not credited by the masses. Attack by an unfriendly nation seemed far more on the cards — Yet there were no airplanes to account for the ever-louder droning. It was as though a mighty swarm of locusts were on the move.

Then the attackers were seen in the grey light — a cloud so black it extended for miles, at a height of perhaps five or eight hundred feet. Insects, gigantic ones, of every known type that could fly, and many others that were unidentifiable. Instantly the alarms rang throughout the country, throughout Europe, throughout various regions of the eastern United States.

The bee-cum-wasp which the Reverend

Horace Hancock had fought was there again, duplicated tens of thousands of times. By five o'clock that morning London was suddenly enveloped in the hurtling monsters. Directed by a central intelligence, presumably that of the ants themselves at present out of sight, the flying horrors with their deadly barbs of venom, swooped upon and destroyed every human they could spot. They hurtled over buildings, between them, along the streets at low level, manoeuvring with a speed and accuracy denied to any aircraft. Early workers fled for shelter. Those who were not quick enough were stabbed and killed instantly.

London and its environs, almost before it realized it, was in the midst of the strangest onslaught it had ever known In many ways the attack was ill-timed for most of the people were indoors — or at least it seemed ill-timed to commence with. All sources of authority got on the move within the safety of buildings and orders went out to the air force and militia to deal with the situation.

By nine o'clock the battle had begun

— aircraft versus ever thickening clouds of vast giant wasps, and for every insect that was destroyed half a dozen more swept in to take its place. The supply of reserves seemed inexhaustible, and the source from which they came quite undetectable.

With complete disregard for themselves the flying horrors smashed windows and hurtled into the inside of buildings, wiping out with their venom the frantic human beings inside. In the street traffic was at a standstill, or else being blown to bits as bombs rained down from the circling aircraft. In the main it seemed to be the aircraft that were getting the worst of it. Time and time again the hornets were sucked into the jet motors. Thicker whirled the insects, and thicker still, blotting out the sunlight with their endless hordes and blanketing over London like a living snowstorm.

Slow and inevitable paralysis was coming. By noon smaller insects had arrived. They cloaked the buildings so thickly it was impossible to see the masonry. They crawled through windows, under doors, into cracks. They drove humans into the streets where they were pounced upon and slaughtered. It was a situation rapidly getting beyond all control.

Len Chalmers was as much mixed up in the battle as any other able-bodied man. Upon the sounding of the alarm he had reported instantly to his nearest unit and he spent the morning in a gun-pit doing his best with the men around him to shoot down the swarming fliers blackening the summer sky. He wondered vaguely amidst the confusion how Nick and Ena were faring, and the more he thought about them and the uselessness of his own present position, the more he realized that he ought to get in touch with them. They, like hundreds of other people in the outlying districts, would be utterly unprotected. Here, in the city, there were at least the defence forces to help matters . . .

So Len left his post without leave and began to make his way through the embattled streets towards his own home again. But he never reached it. It was just as he came to the end of the street, with its cluttered up masses of fallen insects and sweating, fighting men that the earthquake came. There was no warning, save a deep rumbling growing ever louder — then Len felt as if the ground suddenly came up and hit him.

Plunged into the gutter he dragged himself to his knees and looked around him in horrified amazement. London was rocking to its depths. The taller buildings, with their clinging millions of smaller destructive insects, were overbalancing and hurling their masonry into the clogged streets, burying men and dying insects indiscriminately. The roadways began to split in twain, dropping the fighting units into depthless canyons. Out of these canyons came dense smoke from internal fires.

Windows that had survived the battering of the hornets now smashed completely in warping facades. In other parts of the city the Underground entrances sloughed downward in whirling clouds of sulphuric smoke, burying the few troop trains under countless tons of masonry. Ships at anchor in the river were swamped and smashed in an onrushing tidal wave. In the space of a few minutes, as it all seemed, all London was transformed. It fell like a pack of cards and wiped out tens of thousands in the process.

Len, for his part, found himself caught up in a screaming mob of men, women, and children. Already at breaking point from the attack of the insects, this new horror had driven them to absolute panic. All order and reason had gone. They streamed out of the shattering buildings and into the streets, preferring to brave the attacks of the flying insects to being crushed to death. Amongst these terror stricken hordes Len was borne along helplessly, his ears filled with the din of collapsing buildings and subsiding earth, his eyes blurred with dust and continuously rolling smoke.

Somehow, he survived. With the cessation of the earthquake he found himself at an unfamiliar part of the city, surrounded by the now somewhat calmer survivors.

The day had become well advanced, the undisturbed late afternoon sunlight pouring its saturating heat on a scene of indescribable chaos.

The only bright spot in the whole ghastly business seemed to be that the invader had mysteriously disappeared, The sky was clear and the shattered buildings had not a single insect upon them. Recalled by the governing intelligence behind them the army had vanished . . . Until the next move.

Len spent his time until nearly ten that night helping to move the dead and dying. Then he snatched some brief sleep, awoke to have a meal from a few salved provisions, and went to work again amidst the ruins with the rescue parties. By the time dawn came again the survivors were able to take stock.

From the trickle of news brought by other survivors it seemed that London had succumbed to a gigantic underground fault. It had not been so much an earthquake as a fault deep below the surface — a colossal cave-in, which had torn the city up by the roots. Some were even satisfied with this explanation and forgot the preceding attack by the hornets. Len, able to think further, was anything but satisfied. He viewed it all as a plan being worked out with inhuman cunning. But, since he had nobody around him with the intelligence to understand, he kept quiet,

As no further attacks seemed to develop he made an effort to try and locate some surviving scientists — and failed. He could not even discover where the Entomological Institute had been. So, as the morning advanced, he decided to strike out southwards and try and locate Nick and Ena, if they still lived. Perhaps conditions there might not be so chaotic as in London.

He made a move which was probably providential for it was just as he had reached the outermost limits of the shattered city that he sighted the advancing hordes of termites . . . He could not believe his eyes for the moment but the instant he did he ducked down behind a monstrous pile of masonry and watched intently.

They were advancing from the east, most of them moving upright on their rear appendages. Len estimated there were probably a thousand of them, every one quite nine feet high covered in deep red shell, stalked eyes and investigating antennae waving as they moved. The fact that they were carrying queer-shaped weapons in their tentaculate hands made it obvious that their intelligence was of a high-order — probably far above that of the human. Soldier ants, every one of them evidently bent on consolidating the gains they had achieved so far.

Len kept out of sight, just far enough out of range of the hordes to escape notice, and since he felt no mental disturbance he assumed the soldier ants were either too far away to cause trouble, or else they had not the gift of hypnosis like the directing intelligence behind them.

Len got on the move again, and half an hour later he had reached the open country. Ahead of him, in various directions, loomed the huge piles of termitaria but they seemed to be harmless enough with no ants or other insects in sight He went on steadily, thankful for the warmth of the sun and the brief peace that had descended.

# 6

## Invaders from Time

It was late afternoon when Len came within sight of The Cedars and to his relief he beheld it still as it had always been — as was the house on the hill. In fact the village did not seem to have been touched. Len kept on going and at last, weary from his long journey, was hammering on the front door of the big residence. As he waited he glanced about him at the distant termitaria, silent in the hot sunlight.

The door opened. Ena stood there, pale-faced, drawn-looking but she did manage a welcoming smile. 'Len! The last person we ever expected to see again — '

She shook hands warmly and led the way into the big lounge. Nick was there, busily assembling a pile of oil-soaked tree-branches into the empty fireplace. He stopped working as Len came in and rose to shake hands.

'Glad you're still alive, Len,' he said sombrely. 'We were wondering about you.'

'You know, then, what happened in London?' Len sank down into a chair.

'Yes. Some of the radio reports kept on going, probably from mobile transmitters, and we heard all about the hornet attack and the earthquake. Not that the hornet attack was any surprise to us. We saw it fly over us in the direction of London.'

'You were not attacked then?'

'Not by the hornets. But six termites did their best to get us out of here: they came from the nearest of the termitaria outside there. Fortunately this is a well-built place and we defeated them. We poured boiling water on them from the upper windows and flung lighted wood into their faces. They retired finally. Those in the village weren't so lucky.'

'I doubt,' Ena said, pushing back her hair wearily, 'if a single person in the village has survived. A horde of some hundred ants attacked it early today. We caught a glimpse of men, women, and children being carried along to that termitarium you can see through the window. It must have some kind of hidden door in it for the men and women and children were bundled through it, and the termites followed. I suppose, by now, they will be dead.'

'Which accounts for the peacefulness of the village as I passed through it,' Len muttered. 'I had assumed that nothing had happened. Evidently the peace was caused by everybody having been abducted.'

Silence. Then Ena stirred to life again. 'I'll fix up a meal for you, Len,' she said. 'You must need it after all you've been through.'

She left the lounge and Nick gave a grim look. He nodded towards the oil-soaked woods in the fireplace.

'In readiness,' he explained. 'I'm pretty well sure the brutes will attack again.'

'Nothing more certain,' Len confirmed. 'We're at the start of a very grim chapter in mankind's history, Nick — the struggle between the insect world and human beings. Whoever is beaten will become the slaves of the victor . . . And from the way things have started I'm afraid humanity has had its day.'

Nick frowned. 'But you can't mean that, man! Look at the weapons we have got, the science we understand, the — '

'The termites have weapons, and they have a science of their own, too. What do you suppose they have been doing all these months whilst nothing happened? Preparing! And how thoroughly they have done it! Those endless hordes of giant hornets utterly destroyed morale in the city. It was simply impossible to fight them: they were in such numbers. And they are blindly obedient to the master-mind directing them.'

'Then — they'll go further?'

'No doubt of it. When I left London hundreds of soldier ants were marching in to deal with the survivors. I managed to escape. The position in this country is desperate, Nick. How it is in other countries I don't know. Probably the radio could tell us.'

'I've had one or two reports,' Nick responded. 'There didn't seem to be anything definite at that time. Most of the information concerned the things happening in London. Fortunately I have a battery-receiver otherwise we'd have no radio at all in this one-eyed place. And the battery won't last forever, either. I don't suppose I'll ever get it charged up again with things as they are.'

Ena returned carrying a meal on a tray. She set it out on the table.

'The water will be boiling soon for some tea,' she said. 'Takes a bit of time on the oil stove. When the oil runs out I don't know what we'll do. We've used a lot for the torches.'

'You're a kind soul,' Len said, smiling tiredly as he settled at the table. 'And you're not very convincing, either of you. All three of us are talking irrelevancies because we don't dare say what we're really thinking. Right?'

Nick nodded and Ena shrugged.

'You're the only one likely to know what is going to happen next, Len,' Nick remarked.

'That being so I'll tell you what I think. I believe that in the interval of time the giant ants have honeycombed this Earth of ours inside, as low as they can get, have turned it into a mighty termitarium for their own uses. I arrive at that conclusion because they produce their exterior termitaria at all parts of the globe with equal ease, which means they have free movement from one side of the globe to the other below surface. I also think the surface termitaria are only blinds — seventy five percent of them anyway. Just dummies. Which is why I suggested we stop bombing them. They don't mean a thing. They are merely there to distract our attention from what might be going on elsewhere. Here and there, there are genuine openings, of course, like the one near here into which the village inhabitants were herded.'

Ena departed for a moment to make the tea. She returned with it and set it down. Len went on eating and then continued.

'Another thing which I do not think was genuine was that London earthquake. We're not in the earthquake zone in England — not to that extent anyway. I believe London has been hollowed out underneath and at a given moment the props — whatever they may be — were removed which brought the city down.'

'But how on earth could a whole city the size of London be propped up?' Nick asked incredulously. 'It's utterly impossible!'

'By ordinary means, yes — but not by *scientific* means. I should think force beams, or degravitators, might be the explanation.'

'But we're dealing with *ants*!' Ena protested. 'You speak of them as if they were exceptionally clever humans. They are only insects when you've said and done all.'

Len sighed. 'When will you and Nick understand — when will anybody understand — that we're not dealing with insects, but with extremely clever scientists who happen to have the bodies of insects! That is the only difference — in their physical appearance. Otherwise they have fully evolved brains backed by fifty million years of evolution. The ordinary ant is quite scientific in the way it does things. Now it has achieved full size it will put all those scientific accomplishments into practice. The fact that they understand biological surgery is clearly evidenced by the myriads of giant hornets they have produced and — '

Len stopped, his ear cocked at a sudden sound. He had no sooner become aware of it than there was a sudden shattering of glass and the French windows crashed open. On the threshold, against the golden light of the afternoon, stood a giant red soldier ant, a weapon in its tentaculate hand. Its compound eyes glared with fiendish ferocity.

For perhaps ten seconds the trio gazed in amazement — then Nick lunged to the fireplace for the torches he had piled there. Before he could complete his action the instrument in the ant's claws flashed at him with a purple beam. He staggered helplessly and then fell to the carpet.

'Nick!' Ena screamed in horror, racing across to him. 'Nick — !'

The beam got her too. It did not kill, she found. It simply destroyed all her power of movement. Her legs went to the consistency of water and she dropped helplessly on her face and remained still, quite unable to move a finger.

Len sprang up, snatching up the teapot. He hurled it unerringly at the ant, noticing as he did so that other ants were coming up in the rear. In fact the grounds of the big residence seemed to be thick with them.

The teapot rebounded from the creature's scaly head and its mandibles clicked in fury as the boiling liquid cascaded over it — then it retaliated savagely with its weapon. Len's body gave way and he pitched helplessly beside Ena, completely petrified. He could hear everything, and see everything too as far as his head was positioned, but to move or even blink was impossible.

There was the rustling and shifting of insectile feet as the termites came into the lounge. Between them they raised the helpless three and carried them outside, across the grounds of the house, then over the field beyond. Since they were not able to see where they were going, being carried so their eyes were directed at the sky, the trio had no idea how the side of the nearby termitarium was opened. They only knew they were borne within it and, for a time at least, found themselves carried in semi-darkness. They seemed to be in a long rocky tunnel. They could dimly see the rough roof overhead. Light, wherever it came from, was concealed — and therefore indirect.

The journey ended after perhaps half a mile of advancement and the three were set down. Even as the action was performed they began to find the paralysis, evidently only of a temporary nature, was wearing off. After a while it passed altogether and they sat up and looked at one another in the dim light.

'What's — what's happened?' Ena asked in bewilderment. 'Where are we? If it comes to that why are we still alive?'

'I don't think we shall be for long,' Len answered grimly, scrambling up. 'Least we can do is try and find out what this place is. Some kind of underground cavern, I imagine. And evidently we can't escape or we wouldn't have been left to our own devices like this.'

The three very soon discovered that there was very good reason for them having been left to do as they wished. They were inside a cavern with four encircling walls and no sign of a door. There must have been one somewhere, but the termites had evidently closed it when they had departed. There was, however, a roughly circular window driven through the rock, thick bars embedded in it. Immediately Len moved to it, drawn by the glow of light visible beyond it. He caught his breath at what he beheld.

An immeasurable distance below was a shifting mass of white lights, an immense and incredible sea of dots Steady gazing by the trio revealed that the lights were not actually moving: they only seemed to because of the vibrations of the air currents which intervened. There was a city down there, of unknown dimensions, and it was possibly at the unheard depth of four or even five miles.

'What do you make of it?' Nick asked at length. 'How the devil was all this hollowing out accomplished?'

'By scientific means, obviously — though I must admit I am a bit baffled.' Len turned away from the window and stood thinking. 'I know the termites are intelligent, but what is commencing to mystify me is where they got all the scientific apparatus necessary to perform such things as they have done. In a very short time they have converted the interior of our planet into something resembling a rock sponge — a colossal termitarium of planet-sized dimensions — '

'Nick! Len!' Ena exclaimed urgently, as she still peered through the barred window. 'Look here — '

The two men joined her and, imitating her example, they angled their heads sideways so that they could obtain a view outside which had formerly been denied them. It enabled them to see a short length of ledge, from which there opened a fairly well-lighted cavern. It was stacked to the roof with bodies — human bodies! Just like a colossal abattoir's storehouse. Some of the bodies were even hanging on hooks as carcases might hang in a butcher's shop, men, women, and children — some of them moving in anguish but unable to free themselves.

'It's — ghastly!' Ena whispered, yet she was unable to tear her gaze away. 'Do you suppose something like that is going to happen to us?'

Neither Nick nor Len answered her. They had the feeling that it was distinctly possible such a fate could befall them so they were not inclined to enlarge on its likelihood.

'I'm going to see if I can find out what's happened,' Len said. 'That nearest man is within earshot, I think. I'll try.'

He cleared his throat and then called in a bated whisper:

'Can you hear me? I'm in the cavern next to yours. What's happened to you poor people there?'

The man, transfixed by barbs driven ruthlessly through his bleeding wrists, turned his head slowly. He could hardly speak

'Termites . . . ' he gasped. 'We are . . . meat for them. These others died . . . as we shall.'

He could not speak any further, but his meaning was obvious enough. Len turned away, pinching finger and thumb to his eyes.

'It's all too fantastically horrible!' he declared. 'The giant termites are evidently carnivorous, not content with the honeydew of the small species. The only flesh they consume is evidently human, just as we consume cattle. That is quite understandable even if it is horrible. Rather than taint the flesh they will later use for food they kill these people by hanging them — crucifying them if you like — until they die of pain and exhaustion. Any other method might leave toxins in the body and make it unusable. I think we are just beginning to see what this insect menace means. We are just cattle for the new overlords of the planet . . .'

'Can't — can't we get out?' Ena demanded desperately. 'We can't die like that — like those poor people.'

'They're probably villagers, or people taken from London's ruins,' Len mused, then answering Ena's question, he added,

'I just don't see what we can do to help ourselves, Ena. We are not armed, and these termites have highly scientific weapons for use against us — '

He broke off. Suddenly one gigantic wall of the cavern had slid aside, permitting reflected light to pour in from beyond. In the opening stood the giant termites, advancing slowly until they became visible to the three waiting by the further wall. Ena gripped Nick's arm tensely and he murmured a few words of encouragement, Len stood quite still, his fists clenched and his jaw taut. This looked like the end of the road —

For perhaps the first time it was possible to view the termites at close quarters, to study them. Their faces were extremely lengthy and narrow, glistening rather than glazed chocolate of a highly reddish colour. In the midst of the face was a snout-like appendage, and on either side of it the monstrous stalked eyes covered with facets like those of a fly. The bodies were long, sloping to a point at the back and ending about a foot from the floor. The legs, covered in fine hair, terminated in viciously sharp claw-like appendages the foremost ones resembling hands. Last of all came the antennae, the weird natural 'receiving aerial' for telepathic commands issued by the governing intelligence.

'What are we doing standing here like damned fools?' Nick muttered suddenly. 'I'm going to make a dash for it!'

Len tried to stop him — too late. Nick hurtled forward towards the cavern opening, which was left free now that the ants had moved inwards, but he was overtaken instantly by a pulpy yet incredibly strong body that hurled him to the floor. As on the previous occasion paralysing beams took the life out of him and there was nothing more he could do. The same instruments were brought to work again on Len and Ena — then other instruments came into being, which spoke of the baffling brilliant scientific accomplishments of this deadly termite race.

The trio found themselves moved by the simple process of being forced to rise in the air, the only explanation being a series of radio levitating waves generated from a source unknown, which again raised the question: How had the termites gathered together the equipment for such amazing feats of science?

In this floating fashion, the termites behind them, the three drifted down unearthly-looking galleries, slid through softly lit caverns, dropped with the horrible sensation of a falling dream down what seemed infinite miles of shafting, until at last they came within visible range of the city they had seen through the window of their cavern-cell.

Still they drifted, coming ever nearer the lambent haze, until it began to blur and distort like something seen through a curved mirror. Oddly, swiftly, it veered off into nowhere and was replaced by the gleaming interior of a tremendous hall, composed entirely of shining, crystalline metal.

Gradually the floating ceased and the trio discovered they were standing on their feet with paralysis leaving them. They stood close together, watching. Behind them, now clearly visible in the strange pallor, loomed the soldier-termites — more hideous than ever. And in front, inexplicable and complex, were machines of almost translucent texture reflecting the unknown shadowless light in a million varieties of bewildering and yet lovely colour.

Then presently, out of the haze of glory, there appeared another ant, similar in appearance to the soldier-ants, only far larger, It halted before the trio, glaring stalked eyes fixed on them, its hand-like tentacles resting on a small wheeled-machine. It moved a button. Instantly its thoughts came battering into the brain of the trio, so violently they almost staggered as if from a physical blow. Immediately the termite cut down the power.

'I am the queen ant, the central intelligence . . . '

This seemed to be the gist of the thoughts conveyed, and of course the thoughts were transposed into the only language that made sense to the trio — English.

'You may consider yourselves more fortunate than your fellows in escaping death — for the moment — because you,

Chalmers, happen to be the first scientist we have captured. And your two companions are included in your own safety. Fortunately, the barrier of time and body makes no difference to our communicating. With this machine your brains are rendered malleable for my particular thought-vibrations. If you wish to answer, just speak: the concentration behind the words will be sufficient for me. I realize you are wondering upon the strangeness of things?'

'I am more than wondering,' Len answered. 'I am completely baffled. I know that the giant termites have powerful intellects and possibly the wherewithal to create certain scientific instruments — but I certainly do not understand the vast science visible in this underworld, or the high peak of intelligence to which you have attained.'

'The answer to that, Chalmers, is that we are not the termites of your own time.'

Len looked even more bewildered and exchanged a puzzled look with Ena and Nick.

'Not of our time?' Len repeated. 'Then

— then where do you come from?'

'From the year 6960, nearly five thousand years ahead of you. Time in which the giant ants created by Cyrus Odder and Dr. Royd have evolved, to become the mighty scientific race you see around you. We are the undisputed masters of time, space, and matter.'

'But what happened to the giant ants which flourished from the eggs of the original giant ants?' Len demanded.

'They went underground, naturally, but there were only a few thousand of them. We, who are always investigating Time and the events happening therein, found that they had recorded on our instruments, which seemed an unbelievable thing. It meant that termites as gigantic as ourselves — but with nothing like our range of knowledge — had actually come into being nearly five thousand years before we had reached the apex of our development. They must be the products of an experiment, and not the outcome of natural evolution. Our records show that humans did not become dominated by the ant world until around the year 6890, so how came these giant termites in a much earlier period? We decided to investigate and sent scouts into past Time to study the position. We learned that these ants were in truth the progeny of a scientific experiment that meant that they were also the beginning of our race, we having stemmed from them in succeeding centuries to reach the peak we hold in 6960. Do you understand what I am telling you?'

'Hazily,' Len replied. 'You mean the ants of the two who were blown to bits were actually the basis of the giant ant race who, with the passage of centuries, gained enough power to overthrow humanity around the year 6890?'

'Exactly so. We of 6960 decided that we might send half our numbers back in Time and begin the conquest of humans much earlier than records have put it. So we came, bringing with us scientific instruments. We created this city; we brought all insects under our control, and we absorbed all the giant ants of this age under our control.'

'Apparently you don't know much

about Time,' Len remarked. 'You are trying to alter a state of affairs which, to you has already happened. And it can't be done.'

'It can — because there are two states of Time. The abstract and the real. There are also many lines of Time development starting from one source — just as many destinations at the end of a railway line can be reached from a common departure platform . . . We intend to take over this planet, Chalmers, four thousand years ahead of the stated period, and so far we have been very successful. Our science is immense, our organization perfect. Further, we need humans for fodder.'

Len became thoughtful, then finally he said,

'I still cannot reconcile your notions on Time. You are here before your birth! That is impossible!'

'Not at all. Time is a circle, therefore we are not before our birth, but after our deaths. Is there anything else you wish, as a scientist, to know before you die? I am granting the privilege of explanation because you are a scientist, a privilege which your friends are sharing.'

Len was silent, his face grim. Finally he shook his head. He knew he was beaten. The queen ant made a motion with her tentacle and the remaining ants immediately went into action. The paralysers and radio-lifting beams came into operation once more and the trio found they were guided, quite helplessly, through the complex machine rooms of the termite city. When at length they were permitted to have their faculties again they realized they were within a grim-looking apartment, hooks outjutting from the metal walls in a manner horribly reminiscent of the human storage cavern they had seen earlier.

'Nick, they're not going to — ?' Ena's voice choked with fear as she watched one of the termites pull down the hooks on a ratchet device.

'I think we might do worse than try and make a dash for it,' Len murmured, glancing at the termites to the rear. 'It's better to be killed outright than crucified — *Now!*'

At that he jumped forward with Nick behind him, abruptly swinging back on his tracks. With like speed the hideous insects closed in a circle, paralysing beams flashing. Nick felt that sapping enervation at his nerves and muscles and he began to collapse weakly to the floor. Just as suddenly however, the effect vanished. In surprise he looked upward and what he saw jolted the life back into him again,

Standing in the doorway of the storage room was a girl — the merest wisp of a creature, lightly attired in a flowing sleeveless costume, which gleamed like cloth-of-gold. Her bare white arms were pleasantly rounded; her black hair dropped to her shoulders in rippling waves.

Len, also looking at her, got the impression that she was fairly beautiful, but had hardly time to verify his conclusions just then. His gaze only glanced over her youthful face and then dropped to her small hand. In it, held with absolute steadiness, was a small but efficiently designed instrument.

Evidently it possessed considerable

power for the termites were already backing away in manifest uneasiness.

'Where on Earth did this girl come from?' Ena asked in wonder.

At Ena's remark the girl beckoned the three towards her. When they had reached her side she indicated that they were to follow her. Then she slowly began to withdraw from the doorway. Once she had got completely beyond it she started running at a tremendous speed, tirelessly, unerringly, through the complex tunnels and galleries of the vast anthill. On the way the three, panting and running to the rear, passed a cavern filled with gigantic electrical machinery which left Nick and Ena, at least, completely baffled.

'I should imagine they're the engines for the force and radio beams,' Len said, as Nick remarked upon them whilst running. 'Not that I'm interested at the moment: I'm wondering where this girl's heading.'

That the termites were in pursuit seemed more than likely, but under the girl's twisting turns, side-stepping movements, and journeys down unexpected galleries, the termites were finally thrown off and the sound of their insectile feet upon the rock floor died away. The girl came to a halt at last in a vast and gloomy cavern, light reflecting into it from outside. She looked at the three, her still somewhat immature bosom rising and falling steadily with hard breathing.

'You talk my language?' she asked, and though she spoke perfectly it was with tremendous rapidity. The language was English but with the words flowed together in the queerest fashion.

'We're Britishers — ' Len began, but the girl cut him short with a quick nod.

'I know — like the others in the storage rooms. I was brought from 6890 as fodder, along with many others. My name is Arona, and I am a daughter of the human ruler of my age. I was captured by mistake before the big termite exodus to this earlier Time. Usually the high born of the humans are left untouched. I have been here a long while. Just now, when my termite guard fell asleep, I managed to get this ithania-gun from his belt.'

She paused, indicating the instrument in her hand, and then continued, 'This is a very deadly weapon. It changes matter into energy, I dissolved my prison door with it. On my way to escape I came across you. Being humans like myself I saved you. Now I have work to do. No time to lose.'

'What's your plan?' Len asked quickly.

'I have a scheme whereby I can release my race from bondage to the termites in 6890. As you probably know, the termites of that Age have subjected the human race as they propose to do in this much earlier time. If we could be free of them we would be lords of the world again. In 6890 there are five thousand termites left behind to guard the humans. Suppose one of their number came from here, called on the reserves, and emptied the underworld? That would leave humans free! We could then start again and leave all the termites trapped in this age.'

Len rubbed his chin. 'Which wouldn't

be so nice for the people of our Time, Arona.'

'Humans here greatly outnumber the termites,' she answered. 'I know that for a fact. Once the termites are trapped here I will see to it that my father provides the humans of your surface with machinery and weapons sufficiently powerful to wipe out the insect menace.'

'But,' Nick put in, 'whilst these termites have got time-machines and understand time travel, they can always get back to 6890.'

'But they don't understand time travel!' Arona insisted. 'It was my *father* who discovered that. Only he knows the real secret behind it, and he retains it in spite of termite threats. They do not dare do much to him because his knowledge is so useful. If the machines here are destroyed the termites will never be able to get back to 6890.'

'Well, all right,' Len agreed finally, after thinking it out. 'We may as well fall in with your plans, Arona, because we certainly can't do anything on our own. But how do you propose to snare the ants from your age to this one? What ant is going to give the order for reserves?'

'I shall be the ant,' the girl answered simply; then as the three stared at her blankly she motioned for them to follow her again.

# 7

## Arona's sacrifice

It became more than obvious to the trio as they followed the girl through the weird convolutions of the planet-sized termitarium that she was working to some kind of prearranged plan,

Progress continued at good speed, and yet with caution, through galleries that were unknown to the three but obviously familiar to Arona — until at last they emerged into a cavern stacked with all manner of strange machinery, illuminated by a pulsing red light not unlike neon. Here Arona turned in her quick, bright fashion.

'See that?' she asked, and she pointed to a machine not entirely unlike an electric chair — or perhaps an electric bed would have been nearer the mark. It was a long stretcher of crystalline substance with a queerly-fashioned helmet at one end, from which there snaked thick wires leading to a generator, and other quite incomprehensible electrical equipment.

'Upon that rests my hopes,' she continued. 'Termites, as you may know, even in this Age, are amazingly resourceful. Imagine, then, their power in 6890! When the body of one of their numbers — usually a neuter or soldier ant — gets out of action or badly hurt, but the brain remains unimpaired, his entire brain is changed instantly to another termite carcass from which the brain has already been removed . . . '

'Just like Uncle Cyrus did,' Ena put in quickly, and after a puzzled glance Arona continued:

'The body, of course, has not withered. It can be preserved in solution for an indefinite time, but the brain which formerly tenanted it has probably suffered irreparable injury and been destroyed. So, the instant change of brain from one body to the other provides that ant with a new body with which to carry on life. The process is entirely four-dimensional surgery. The brain is transferred without ever once coming into contact with anything material in transit: it is simply rotated through hyperspace to its new home. Every part of the operation is automatic and accomplished by the movement of a masterswitch beside the stretcher-table here. I happen to know because I've seen the operation many, many times.'

'Well?' Len asked quickly.

'In the next cavern are some five hundred termite bodies waiting to be used for brain transference in case of damage to any of the workers. The place isn't guarded: like everything else in this machine anthill it is automatically controlled. Besides, there is no need to guard it. I'm going to get one of those ant bodies and transfer my brain into it, afterwards putting my own body in the solution that contained the ant, until I shall need to transfer back again.'

'So,' Arona finished, 'if in my own Time I encounter other termites — as I shall — my real identity will not be known. My call for reinforcements will appear genuine. I know the termites' telepathic language, of course. Now do you see?'

'And what happens to us?' Ena asked. 'Once we have lost your protection we'll soon be imprisoned or killed.'

'You will come with me — as my captives.'

'Into — into Time, you mean?' Ena's blue eyes went wide.

'Certainly. You have no reason to fear the journey.'

There was a silence. Then finally Len cocked his eye on Nick and Ena and found them nodding slowly. He looked back at Arona's anxious face.

'You're taking a terrific chance, Arona,' he said. 'As regards yourself, I mean. We are quite willing to come with you, but how do you know that your brain will link up properly with that of a termite body, which must be constitutionally different?'

'I don't.' Arona gave a little shrug. 'But since the formation of an insect-brain in 6890 is almost identical with that of a human I see no reason to anticipate failure. In any case I have got to try.'

She turned away quickly and the three followed her into the adjoining cavern. With some difficulty they removed the heavy body of a brainless neuter from an airtight cylinder of solution, and then dragged it along the floor to the specially designed trestles beside the complicated surgical bed.

Finally Arona climbed on to the bed itself, lay down on her back, and fitted the helmet into position on her head, afterwards adjusting a complicated mechanism on the skull of the insect close beside her. Once this was done her arm reached out and deflected the master switch of the amazing surgical instrument.

From that moment onwards the three who stood watching were the astounded observers of the most incredible surgery. The girl's young body relaxed gently under the anaesthetic automatically infusing into her bloodstream, Her eyelids closed and her breathing stopped completely.

Still the clicking mechanisms continued working. Strange tubes began to glow brightly; ripples of violet light passed through inexplicable cylinders of transparent metal. From start to finish the operation probably lasted ten minutes

— then the heavy, ugly body of the neuter ant began to twitch and vibrate. The surgical machine stopped. With heavy movements the ant dropped from the trestles.

'I don't believe it!' Nick declared, staring blankly. 'It just *can't* be!'

But after a moment or two he, Ena, and Len were all forced into admitting that the miracle had happened, The girl's brain had been transferred through a four-dimensional medium into the carcass of the ant. Now, though she was unable to speak, she explained most of her wishes by actions.

Her own limp and apparently dead body was taken from the table and placed in position in the solution cylinder that had formerly held the ant. The whole thing — particularly to Len, who had conceived more than a mere liking for the girl from 6890, was decidedly nightmarish. He took charge of the girl's body and he felt convinced as he lowered the slender figure gently into the strange liquid that he was in the midst of some devilish dream. But he also noticed that holding the body, lifeless though it was, had a decided attraction for him.

Finally, his task done, he returned to where the ant, Nick, and Ena were waiting. His glance was questioning — so the ant — Arona — jerked her insectile head and began to move.

From then onward the party continued its harrowing journey through the galleries, Len, Nick, and Ena beginning to feel almost exhausted by the constant strain of events and lack of nourishment —

Then their spirits began to rise somewhat at beholding ahead of them a fleet of perhaps fifty cylindrical machines resting in an immense open space, guarded over by two watchful soldier termites.

Arona paused and motioned the trio to go ahead of her whilst she came up in the rear with the ithania-gun in her tentaculate hand. It certainly gave the impression that the three from the surface were captives — and evidently Arona's mental communication with the guards satisfied them too for the three were permitted to enter the airlock of one of the gleaming strangely designed cylinders, after which they found themselves in a control room.

Arona followed them in and the airlock closed. She crossed to the switchboard and her tentacle-hands moved the controls.

Almost instantly the motors hummed and the view outside suddenly reeled away into the hazy mist of intervening Time.

For a while Arona gazed at the exterior view, then evidently satisfied she crossed to a machine similar to the one the queen termite had used. Under its influence her thoughts immediately became appreciable to the trio.

'While this task is undertaken,' came her mental message, 'you will, as I explained before, apparently remain as my prisoners. That is the only method by which I can explain away your presence. Leave the rest to me. In roughly thirty of your ordinary minutes the five thousand year gap in Time will have been bridged. None of you must say anything: just leave everything to me.'

The three nodded promptly and as

Arona switched off they turned their attention to the windows, to behold nothing but the blank void of intervening years.'

'Wonder how this Time-travel business is accomplished?' Nick asked, rubbing the back of his head. 'I've read plenty of theories, but I certainly never expected to try it out first hand. The bit I cannot get over is that there can be so many lines of Time all springing from one source. I'd always taken Time as being one inevitable line in which everything must repeat.'

'Not necessarily,' Len responded. 'It's as the queen-ant told us: you can move in space to various positions even though you start from the same source. It does not say because you begin a journey from one particular spot that you must finish it at one particular spot. There are alternatives. Since Time is only an abstract variation of space — in that you cannot move in Time without also moving in space — I assume that the same rule applies. How right am I, Arona?' he asked, glancing at the termite.

She moved from the controls and again

switched on her communicating gear. Her mental reply was perfectly clear.

'You have the basis of the idea quite correctly, my friend — but as for explaining in scientific detail how this Time-travelling is accomplished, I just could not. I only utilise certain principles, but I do not understand them. These machines work on the principle of every Time-line — no matter how many alternatives there may be — being circular, divided only by a hypothetical blank time — hyper-space. Electrical frequencies, governing the space, produce a connecting link between a past and future moment, producing finally a continuous movement forward instead of the sporadic advancement of normal Time . . . '

'In essence,' Len said, musing, 'it boils down to the fact that you have found a way of using that eternal riddle of science — the split second of no-Time between one instant and the next.'

'That,' Arona's thoughts agreed, 'would seem to be the case. My father could explain it thoroughly, but I cannot.'

'I think we'll just accept it for what it is,' Ena said, with an uneasy smile. 'It's all too utterly complicated for me!'

So no more was said on the subject, and at length the thirty minutes were up. The switches on the control board were reversed and through the windows began to appear a most unexpected sight — the vision of a city of what seemed to be white stone, carved in blatant angles against a brilliantly blue and sunlit sky. There were ordered streets, uniform squares, beauteous fountains and graceful trees. In fact in every way the metropolis resembled a tropical city of tremendous wealth and power.

'It is deceptive, though,' Arona said, through the communicator, as she read the thoughts of the trio. 'It looks as though it is the ruling city of the world, but it is not. Though populated by human men and women and ruled over by my father, it is the termites below who are the real masters, and have been for so many grim years.'

She moved back to the control board and operated more switches. In response, the machine, which was evidently equipped with necessities for ordinary air travel as well — began to rise afterwards moving towards the lower walk of the stupendous city — and then sinking down into a shaft which was a grey profundity of unknown depth.

Presently the shaft was no longer there. The machine was dropping through absolute emptiness that still possessed the same weird, pearly light. Then there gradually appeared out of the infinity an immense insectile colony very similar to that which had been created in the underworld from which they had moved in Time.

Without pause the flying Time-machine sped over the outermost galleries and ramifications of the expanse, gently halting at last within a mighty cavern. It did not contain anything except one huge machine. Len, at least, recognized the machine as being a remarkably perfect radio-transmitting device, some kind of major-alarm machine, designed probably to radiate its message to the furthest corners of this astounding world of 6890.

To this instrument, once the time machine had come to rest, Arona immediately hurried, flicking the controlling buttons with her quick tentaculate hands. The equipment came into instant life, its massive generators humming powerfully . . . No sound came from Arona's rigid, antlike form, so evidently her communication was mental — but there were other sounds, the deep rumbling of heavy machines on the move, the scrape of myriads of insectile feet, the bustle and rustle of an incredible world suddenly disturbed.

Then Arona abruptly changed the position of one of the control switches and there came into the minds of the watching trio a sudden impression of her thought.

'This shortens the telepathic wavelength to the radius of this transmission cavern, so you can understand me. I have issued orders to all termites, told them to leave for your Age at once, and that upon them getting there depends the safety of their race. I think they will obey. Once they have gone it means the safety of this age — indeed the conquest of the termite menace entirely. In the meantime, until we are sure our plan has succeeded, we can rest. You three must need it, I, in this ant body, do not feel fatigue or the need of food and drink. You will discover both in that wall recess there. It is always there in case of long sessions at this transmitting machine.'

Len hurried immediately to the spot she had indicated and from it withdrew sealed containers of tabloid food, together with tablets which, when they dissolved in the mouth, provided a copious drink. For the next fifteen minutes the three were busy restoring their energy and at the same time resting with their backs against the wall. Arona remained at the opening of the cavern, her ant body in silhouette. She seemed to be listening to the murmur and movement of the myriads on the move.

Nick and Ena both found themselves drowsing. They could not help it after the nourishment they had taken and the vicissitudes through which they had passed. Len, however, kept awake, thinking of many things. The amazing nature of Time, the web of science that had been woven from Uncle Cyrus's amazing experiment, and especially Arona. Back in time, five thousand years prior to this period, was her real body, in a sealed vat. A beautiful body, the body of a girl whom he realized now that he loved intensely —

His thoughts stopped and his eyes switched to the cavern opening. Arona had suddenly stepped back in alarm and at this moment a gigantic male ant appeared. As he came closer his thoughts began to be picked up by the still functioning machine and reflected back to Len. Since Nick and Ena were asleep they did not hear or see a thing.

'So, this is a trick?' The intonation of the termite's thoughts was malevolent. 'You are no neuter — no soldier. I recognise the trend of your thoughts. You are a human! A surface human — like these three around you.'

Arona hesitated for a moment, then her thoughts radiated back again. There was a tremor in them but she held her ground,

'I *am* a neuter, and I have come to

warn you of failure in your Time-conquest of humans unless all of the race leave at once and reinforce our waning army.'

'You lie! Fortunate indeed that I came. You know me well enough — the sub-ruler of this world until our queen returns from conquest. Your disguise does not deceive me. The moment I sensed your telepathic message I became dubious. You will die, and these humans also. As to the others of our race, they will never leave this Age without my permission or the queen's. We will see whether you can gain the mastery by such a childish subterfuge!'

Len did not wait for any more. He had already gathered the danger that threatened. He gave Nick and Ena each a jolt that awakened them, then he vaulted to his feet and flung himself on the monster ant with all his force. But the termite was by far the quicker. He jumped to one side, dodged Len completely, and then clutched Arona. With devastating force he crashed her insectile body to the cavern floor. There followed the horrible sound of cracking limbs under the onslaught, of powerful mandibles snapping hideously. Being still in the machine's radius Arona's anguished thoughts reached the infuriated Len. She was mortally injured, dying, her limbs crushed and broken.

Len wheeled round. The thundering sounds in the great termitarium were mounting. Preparation for departure was still going on — and *would* go on if this over-suspicious monster could be kept quiet.

Even as he was thinking he jumped forward, fingering the unaccustomed switches of the telepathic machine — and more by luck than judgment he snapped it off. Then he seized hold of a mass of hanging wires and pulled violently, tearing them free from their moorings. At least it meant that the monster could not radiate any orders. This was all accomplished in perhaps three seconds, then Len flung himself again upon the shell-like, iron-hard body.

Immediately he realized the impossibility of the fight he had taken on. He was no stronger than a baby in the clutch of the terrible insect. It bent and twisted him without effort, flinging him on the floor with stunning, numbing force.

By this time Nick had shaken the sleep out of his head and scrambled to his feet, but instead of hurrying to Len's assistance he hurtled towards the nearby time-machine. Just for a moment Len, catching a glimpse of him, had the horrifying thought that he was going to try and escape — then he realized how wrong he had been. In a matter of seconds Nick reappeared from the control room, carrying in his hand Arona's deadly ithania-gun.

As Len struggled with increasing weakness in the grip of the ant he saw Nick fiddling with the unaccustomed switch of the gun — then suddenly it worked. A beam speared through the gloom. The edge of an infinitely hot wind scorched Len's face and eyebrows, but the murderous grip fell away from him. Dazed and savagely bruised he found himself lying beneath the remains of the termite — or rather half of it. He had been bisected as neatly as if with a giant knife, the upper half containing his head having become pure energy.

It took Nick a second or two to comprehend the awful power of the weapon he had used, then he dived forward and dragged Len to his feet, at the same time motioning the frightened Ena.

'We've done our job,' Nick said huskily. 'Let's get Arona into the time-machine.'

He, Ena, and Len between them managed to carry the limp body of the neuter into the machine, then Ena slammed the door and locked it. Len rubbed his aching body wearily and Nick moved across to the telepathic machine, using it as he had seen Arona use it.

'Arona,' he asked, 'how do we control this time-machine? What do we do to get back to our own time?'

Arona's thoughts, weak with the pain of her shattered body, came back, Ena supporting her ugly head and Len holding the machine on a tilt towards her.

'I — I am dying,' came her communication. 'My brain is uninjured, but this body is wrecked. You can only save me by

183

getting my normal body back to me. You saw what I did. Simply repeat the operation, but remember that my own body will go on the trestles this time instead of the bed.'

'But — but how do we control this machine?' Nick insisted urgently. 'We don't understand how it operates. What do we *do* — ?'

He was wasting his time. Arona had relaxed completely, her mind a blank. Evidently she had succumbed to her injuries and would remain in this state of semi-death until — or if — her own body was restored to her.

Nick switched off the telepathic machine and gave Len a grim look.

'We couldn't be in a worse mess,' Nick muttered. 'We dare not try and find her father and get him to help us: the termites would be on us in no time. And even if we stay until they have gone to our Age leaving us more or less free, it still won't help Arona. Much more delay and she'll have died in this ant body ... and her own body is in that vat way back in our Time.'

'Have to take a risk, that's all,' Len said, moving to the control board, 'but I'd better raise the machine into the open first because, being underground, we might merge into another Time also in the underground. Since two solids cannot occupy the same space at the same instant there'd be a terrific explosion which might finish us . . . '

He sat for a while examining the layout of the switchboard, then at last he managed at least to figure out how the air control worked. He pressed buttons experimentally and the machine began to move, gliding through the opening in the cavern and afterwards floating high over the vast internal wastes where the termites of 6890 held absolute sway. There were dim signs of vast activity going on down there.

Higher the machine rose, and higher still, and more by luck than judgment Len managed to find the immense central shaft that led up to the surface. The machine emerged at last over the great city that had been the first vision on arriving in this Age. Len brought the machine down to ground level and cut out the power.

'I'm wondering if we should take a chance and try and see Arona's father,' he said, thinking.

Nick shook his head. 'I'm against it. Any moment now the termites may be on their way to our Age and it is possible they will spot us. If they do it will be the end of us and the plot we've worked out to transport them all from this Age. I'm for taking a risk on finding our way back.'

'Okay,' Len said, and again went to work with the switches whilst Nick and Ena watched him tensely.

After a while something worked. There was a click of mechanisms, the hum of the power plant, and then the view outside the windows vanished. There was the blackness of intervening Time. Len sat on, watching the dials with a puzzled expression. The minutes passed in normal time. Outside centuries were shifting.

'How long do we keep going?' Ena ventured. 'Thirty minutes it should be . . . shouldn't it?'

'I don't understand these dials,' Len

replied. 'They work in numerals that don't make sense. I'm not sure whether I'm going backwards or forwards. Maybe I'd better stop.'

He switched off. Outside a view returned. It was redlit and sombre with a range of hills in the distance. Over these hills, bisected by them, hung a gigantic pock-marked sun. Its red rays — about the only rays remaining to it — cast upon sheets of ice that had the colour of blood.

'We're forward, not backward,' Len muttered. 'This is the end of the road nearly — Earth with one face to the sun, the sun nearly burned out, and all life gone.'

He altered the controls immediately the view of the far distant futurity faded out into darkness. The machine was on its way back, utilizing split seconds of no-Time as it shuttled back down the web of untold centuries.

Len was lost, but he would not admit it. He had no idea whatever how to read the instruments, but he did have the hope that by several hits and misses he might gain an insight as to the correct procedure. After perhaps fifteen minutes he came to a halt once more.

Outside it was night. In the far distant an unknown city was blazing with light. In front of it stretched barren plain, Overhead were the stars and gigantic moon.

'Are we before our own Time or after it?' Ena asked, peering through the glass. 'No way of telling.'

'Yes there is,' Len assured her. 'We are still a long way *after* our own Time, even well after 6890. The size of the moon shows it is returning to Earth, and that can only happen in the very distant future . . . I think I have the answer. The thirty minutes is the solution. We've moved back fifteen; if another fifteen brings us to 6890, then thirty more in reverse should return us to our own Time, since that is the period we took before.'

'Which is just what I said!' Ena exclaimed triumphantly, yet inwardly astounded to discover she had hit on a scientific truth.

Evidently the system was correct, though, for after another fifteen minutes, when Len again cut the power, the view was identical to the one they had left in 6980, so with a smile of relief he switched on again and went into reverse for an exact thirty minutes. Then he stopped the engine.

At that instant it seemed as though the Universe came to an end. From outside there belched a terrific explosion — a tearing, shattering concussion which set the time-machine bouncing up and down in the midst of tortured air currents. It took several minutes before the distur- bance finally settled down. He peered outside, Ena and Nick close behind him.

They did not say anything for a while: they were too completely astounded.

# 8

## Aftermath

Apparently the time machine had not come to rest on the surface. It was still below ground. Upon every hand were the galleries of the mighty termitarium, illuminated by the usual indirect lighting. There were also enormous scientific machines, racing themselves to pieces. But there was also a great deal more.

Far below lay the ant-city, swarming with the hurrying insectile forms, all of them heading it seemed towards the already over-jammed space where time machines were lying in ordered rows of cylinders. It was plain from the hordes on the move that considerable numbers had arrived from 6890, probably in the interval whilst Len had made the mistake of travelling into far futurity.

And as the insects moved and teemed in and out of the galleries, travelling with the demoniacal speed that only an ant can achieve, there was a vision of rock and earth crumbling inwards from high in the cavern ceiling.

'What the devil's happening?' Nick panted. 'It looks as if somebody threw an atom bomb in this lot!'

'Something pretty like it,' Len agreed, his eyes narrowed in thought.

He did not say any more for the moment. His attention, like that of Nick and Ena, was centred on the veritable avalanches of rock thundering inwards towards the centre of the enormous cavern, which meant that the time-machine grounds were directly in line. Tens of thousands of tons of rock and earth came smashing from the heights, burying the teeming insects in their struggles, flinging them from the galleries, tumbling over the enormous scientific machines. The city below became the target for an ever-increasing hail of rocks and landfall.

'Do you realize what this means?' Ena asked suddenly. 'These insects can't get back! Their time machines have been wiped out — and thousands of the termites with them! But how did it all *happen*? And just how safe are we?' she added, with an anxious glance around her.

'I've just thought of the explanation,' Len said quickly. 'Our time machine moved in space at the other end — when we went from below to the upper regions. That caused it to move the same distance here, of course. Evidently the surface point in the future is above ground, but the same point here is below it, due to geological formations. What we must have done upon returning here was to merge back *inside* one of the vast gravitational machines used for supporting the surface. One of them was probably used to support London, and then its power was cut off to cause the city to subside. That doesn't signify now. What does signify is that we've exploded equipment that was keeping the surface supported and making this underworld safe. Now the surface is falling inwards and though there must be other gravitational machines they evidently can't cope with the load with one of their number out of action.'

'Then — then you mean the whole *world* is just sagging inwards?' Nick gasped. 'Like — like a mine with the props slowly giving way?'

'That's my guess,' Len agreed tautly. 'If we've done nothing else we've accidentally smashed up these termites. They can't get away into Time, and those that are left are going to be crushed under the avalanche — and so are we if we don't move fast . . . It's Arona I'm thinking of,' he added anxiously, turning back into the control room. 'We've got to get her to that operating room and give her back her body even if the whole planet falls in on us. We're not far from our original position, near as I can judge, so the direction should be straight ahead, then left, right, then left. At least the ants won't bother us. They've enough to do . . . '

'Let's be moving,' Nick said quickly.

He, Len, and Ena all hurried back to the motionless body of the neuter ant that was Arona. They raised the insect and bore it through the airlock, and from then on began their desperate struggle against time and the gradually increasing earth collapse. The only fortunate part was that the ants were all in the lower galleries, deep in the underground city, seeking either protection from the globe-wide avalanche or trying to get to the deeply buried time machines.

Several times in their journey the trio missed their way and had to retrace their steps through the midst of rocks falling from the upper galleries — then abruptly they hit upon the operating room; the lighting was still functioning though it flickered now and again on the verge of extinction.

Immediately the dead body of the ant was dumped on the electric bed and Len headed for the nearby storage room. In the space of a few moments, whilst the walls creaked and groaned and produced fissures at intervals, he had withdrawn Arona's own body from its glutinous preserving solution and carried it to the trestles. He strapped on the helmet and adjusted the mechanism to the head of the termite. Then he depressed the master-switch and waited. The power of the instrument being self contained it functioned immediately.

In the bobbing light Len, Nick and Ena looked at each other fixedly, unable to say anything and feeling particularly helpless in the midst of the surgical miracle proceeding invisibly. As they waited the earth was shaking violently and from outside the cavern there was a constant roaring and rumbling growing ever louder.

As he waited for the surgery to complete its processes Nick found himself wondering what was happening on the surface. The world must be in ruins, one convulsive mass of landslide in which all man's creations must be toppling — but perhaps it was better that way than to have the domination of the termites, now so completely beaten by a scientific accident. At least humans would survive and could probably start again —

But of course they would survive and start again. At least it seemed highly probable since Time itself, in the future, had shown Man to be well away in his upward climb —

'Oh, how in hell much longer?' Len groaned, chafing with impatience — then he looked, round in sudden alarm as part of the cavern ceiling collapsed and left a titanic black hole reaching to apparent infinity.

'Might use that shaft later as a way out,' Ena said breathlessly, peering into the abyss. 'I — I think I can see stars at the top of it — '

She paused as the mechanism controlling the surgical equipment gave a sudden click. The power stopped. For one dreadful moment it looked as though the operation had cut itself short — then Arona began to stir weakly on the trestles. Immediately Len was at her side, holding her head and shoulders in his arms. Simultaneously the waning light expired as power failed in the underworld. The cavern was pitch black and filled with the thunder of rumbling, sliding earth.

'Arona — you're alive? You're all right?' Len insisted, holding her slim, quivering body tightly to him.

'Yes — Yes, I am all right.' Her quick,

natural voice was reassuring. 'Just a bit dizzy from the — But what's happened? I can't see!' There was sudden anxiety in the girl's tone. 'Haven't my eyes connected properly?'

'The whole place is in darkness,' Len answered briefly. 'Better make sure though — Nick, get two bits of rock and strike them against each other.'

'Eh? Oh, sure.'

He fumbled round in the dark, then after a moment or two there was the sound of rock pieces striking each other. For a second there came momentary sparks.

'All right, I saw them,' Arona said in relief. 'Just for a moment I wondered — But what's all the commotion?' she broke off, listening to the booming thunder of a world in anguish.

Len told her as briefly as he could what had been happening. By the time he had finished Arona had completely recovered and found her way from the trestles to the cavern floor.

'Our only chance now is to make use of this huge hole above us,' Len said. 'There are stars visible at the top of it, so at least it leads outwards. Then — '

A truly appalling din drowned out the rest of his words, and with it there seemed to be mingled the screams of termites.

'Sounds like something extra big,' Nick yelled. 'Let's risk a look — '

They found their way to the cavern's opening and, from this high vantage point stared in awe into the depths. There was still an uncertain light cast over the city of the termites and the immediate surrounding area — but the city was sinking downwards in its entirety, carrying with it the immediate territory upon which the ants were scurrying and moving. This also included the space where the time machines were standing. The whole centre of the underworld plateau was dropping — down, down, into tumbling chasms of flame and smoke, carrying the screaming insects with it.

'Internal subsidence,' Len muttered. 'Probably the whole lot is partly degravitated because those insects set normal gravitational laws at zero. Everything down there might go right down to the nickel-iron core itself — '

A violent shaking of the cavern floor got him on the move again. More rock came shattering down from the roof — tons of it in fact, and the quartet dodged back hastily.

'At least it gives us a natural ladder to get into that shaft,' Nick said. 'Sooner we start climbing, the better . . . I'll go first and help up the girls. You can come last and save them if they slip.'

'Okay,' Len acknowledged promptly, and devoted all his attention to Arona as she, following Ena, began the difficult scramble up the rocks in the total darkness.

Nick had been prepared for difficulty, but not for the troubles he *did* encounter. The task of climbing the shaft was not far short of being a mountaineering problem. It demanded struggling from ledge to ledge and using every ounce of muscular power, afterwards to reach down in the void and drag up the struggling girls behind him. They, not possessing masculine muscles, were pretty nearly helpless — but with Len below and Nick above they did manage with painstaking effort to fight their way upwards inch by inch. The greatest danger came from pieces of rock which dislodged themselves and came hurtling down, but in the main they stayed in the shaft centre on their descent and so just missed the climbers.

When they calculated that they had ascended half the distance, and were perched on a ledge recovering their breath, Nick made a comment.

'Maybe we'd have had more sense if we'd tried to get back to the time machine. We could have switched to an earlier time before all this happened.'

'I thought of that,' Len responded. 'But if we'd followed our present Time-line we'd only have come to a point where, later, we would again have to endure the ant menace. And besides, there's no guarantee the time machine is still there. It may have gone down in the general subsidence.'

'If it has,' Arona said slowly, 'and those other machines have gone into the depths — as we know they have — how do I ever get back home?'

Silence, except for the rumble of distant earth subsidences.

'Let's carry on,' Len said, disregarding the girl's question. He could not say outright that the last thing he wished was for her to depart — forever.

So the climb was resumed, ledge by ledge, projection by projection, until at last Nick dragged himself over the edge of the hole and then lay flat, helping up the girls and then Len. They stood, up under the bright stars, a cold early autumn night wind blowing about them.

Arona shivered violently in her flimsy garments, so immediately Len dragged off his jacket and put it about her shoulders; then he held her to him for extra warmth.

'Ruin, ruin, ruin,' Nick muttered, gazing about him. 'There just doesn't seem to be anything else.'

Apparently he was correct. In various directions flames were flickering to the heavens, some of them from the great caverns created in the earth, others from the wreckage of towns. But it did seem that the worst of the subsidence was over for the growling and shaking of the earth had ceased.

'That area over there is probably what's left of London,' Len said finally. 'It's the devil of a distance but I'm afraid it's our only hope. The exercise should keep us warm anyway.'

He began to get on the move, but before very long both Ena and Arona found the going too much for them, so there was nothing else for it but for each man to carry his feminine burden. Nick grumbled somewhat since Ena was no lightweight, but Len seemed to enjoy the task.

'It's possible, Arona,' he said, as he trudged along under the stars with the cold wind flowing about him, 'that you will never find a time-machine with which to return — or rather to go forward — to 6890. We know that the majority of them went down in that central collapse, and the remaining one is somewhere in the underground and by this time may even be buried. Suppose, just for the sake of it, that you never can return to your own age. How then?'

'But — but I must!' she insisted. 'My father will be distracted!'

'He'll be that already, won't he, since he must be aware by this time that the termites captured you in mistake.'

There was a long pause before the girl spoke again, then she said hesitantly.

'It — it wasn't a mistake, Len.'

'Huh? But I thought you said — '

'Yes, I know what I said, but now I'm giving you the facts. I let myself be captured, I wanted to be.'

'But why? You went in danger of your life doing a thing like that.'

'That also was what I wanted. As I told you earlier, the high-born humans back in my age are left unmolested by the termites, yet at the same time they are not permitted any real freedom. Can you imagine what it was like for me, as the daughter of the human ruler? I had everything, and yet I had nothing. No exciting event ever occurred. I might as well have been dead for all the thrills there were, I couldn't stand it. I come of a pioneering, exploring race and the urge in me was too strong to be denied. So, when I knew an excursion into earlier Time was contemplated by the termites, and that they were taking many humans as fodder, I decided to put myself amongst the humans. I took the place of another woman at the last moment and, in the last-minute hurry, my trick went unnoticed. I did it plainly and simply for the adventure — and also to further my plan to be rid of the termites. I mean the plan we put into effect later.'

'Then,' Len said slowly, still tramping steadily and unwilling to admit his back was commencing to ache under the girl's weight, 'if you went back you'd simply return to your former position of inactive eminence?'

'No. Not this time. The termites are destroyed, remember. I would have freedom — as far as my high position permitted. But a high-born person never really *has* freedom.'

'No,' Len admitted, thinking. 'I suppose not . . .'

He hesitated for a long while and then

asked, 'Let's get it clear, Arona. Do you *want* to go back?'

'For the sake of my father's peace of mind, yes. For myself, no. Of course,' Arona finished, 'it is not as if I am his only daughter. I have four sisters who might take the ache out of his heart. I just happened to be the eldest.'

Len began to smile and hugged her more tightly to him.

'I'm thankful that Time does not exist in one straight line but has several alternatives,' he said, 'otherwise this would be impossible. You being five thousand years before the time of your birth, I mean.'

Arona did not answer. The complexities of Time were not uppermost in her mind at that moment. Whether of the present Time or 6890 she was still a young woman — and Len Chalmers was a most likeable young man.

'Be plenty of thrills in this Age for you, anyway,' he remarked at length. 'From what I can see of things the whole of civilisation seems to have come down and it's going to take the toughest and the most intelligent to rebuild it.'

Nick, carrying Ena, began to catch up.

'What are you two talking about so earnestly?' he demanded. 'Or shouldn't I ask?'

'No, you shouldn't,' Ena told him. 'Anyway, you need all your breath to carry me. I think I could do a bit on my own, too, if you put me down.'

Nick promptly did as she suggested, so Arona also elected to move on her own two feet. The journey continued, all four with their arms linked in case one should stumble and the exercise saved them from catching cold in the raw night air.

By the time they had reached the battered outskirts of what they took to be London the dawn had come. It cast a grey, dreary light over skeletons of buildings that had been ravaged by fire and subsidence. There were enormous blank areas filled with smoking rubble and streets seemed to be twisted and out of their original positions. But humanity was not extinct — far from it. Men and women were visible in considerable numbers, most of them in ragged clothes and centred in groups round fires kindled from wreck-age. Towards one of these groups the four made their way.

They were accepted as survivors like the rest of people and given rough food and cans of hot drink. This latter tasted like a cross between soup and tea, but it was acceptable nonetheless.

'Time we found out what has been happening,' Len said, as he settled down with Arona, Ena and Nick on his right. 'Apparently the termites didn't have such a mighty conquest as they expected. There are thousands of human beings in these ruins, and they don't look particu-larly badly done by either. It looks as though the termite conquest wasn't so complete, after all.'

He turned to a bearded man nearby, busy drinking the hot liquid from a can.

'How are things, friend?' he ques-tioned. 'My companions and I got buried below ground and have been out of touch. We know there was a subsidence but — '

'We beat 'em,' the man grinned. 'There are one or two tricks in the bag that even those blasted termites didn't think of — anteaters, for instance.'

Len frowned and, behind him, Arona, Nick and Ena were intently listening.

'Sure. There's an army of them over there, still on the prowl.'

The man nodded into the distant ruins and, turning, the quartet found themselves looking at perhaps twenty remarkable looking animals, each one gigantic in size and having a tail astonishingly like a pile of hay.

'Why, those are anteaters!' Len exclaimed. 'But they inhabit Guiana, Brazil, and Paraguay — and usually they're only about three feet high. Those must each be at least twelve!'

'Sure they are.' The man looked puzzled. 'You mean you don't know what's been happening?'

'Not a thing! We were taken below as fodder, but managed to escape — '

'Oh, thousands were taken below after the big London subsidence,' the man broke in. 'But tens of thousands remained above to do battle, and numerous though the termites were, and backed by scientific weapons, they couldn't possibly capture everybody. Not in every part of the world, that is. Quite a lot of normal life kept on going amidst the ruins, particularly across the Atlantic where the menace hadn't spread to any great extent. I gather the termites aimed at world domination in the finish, but scientists and others across the sea, having advance warning, made their own preparations . . . They enlisted the aid of the termites' most deadly enemy — the anteater. From studying the remains of giant hornets and, insects which were flown to them they found out how the giantism had been produced and immediately used it to enlarge anteaters to the proportions you see here. Scientists by the hundred did nothing else but breed anteaters under forced conditions. *Everything* was thrown into it, making the animals the first line of defence.'

'And then?' Len asked.

'Anteaters were flown in their scores to these embattled regions and turned loose. The termites on the ground, which were all soldiers of course, just did not know what to do. You can't imagine the ferocity of a giant anteater, It tore into every ant with complete disregard for its own safety. True the termites had weapons and they accounted for plenty of anteaters, but their basic morale was destroyed. They had never expected to have to fight ferocious animals. Humans were their game. We, of course, with the anteaters on our side, had a chance, to recover. We opened up with everything we'd got — including atomic and hydrogen bombs. Between us we drove the brutes back into the underworld, and just at that period the second earthquake came. What happened after that I don't know. The whole world seemed to turn inside out, but the termites had gone . . . and they haven't returned.'

'And I don't think they ever will,' Len responded slowly. 'They were sucked down into a volcanic maw, the whole damned lot of them . . . '

He looked across at the group of massive animals with their terrible claws, capable of pulling down any termitarium, and exceptionally long tongues.

'When all comes to all,' Nick said slowly, 'Uncle Cyrus defeated the very menace he started. His trick of turning ants into giants was again used to turn anteaters into giants and they so disorganized the termites that they lost the initiative.'

'Uh-huh,' Len agreed, musing. 'And from the look of things, despite the collapses and ruins, the world is in passable shape even yet. The onslaught must have been checked just in time. We made absolutely sure of finishing the ants by reappearing in this Age so violently and burying the lot of them under crumbling rock. In fact everything worked together for the right answer.'

'And what happens now?' Ena questioned. 'We are little better than savages. Our home may still be standing of course, but we need money, ordinary supplies, all the things that go to make life worth living. How do we even start all over again?'

'Some kind of Government will be formed,' Len assured her. 'Other countries, not as badly hit as ourselves will come to the rescue. In a few months there'll be order coming out of the chaos. As for money — Well, Nick and I can earn some in helping the rebuilding. Eh Nick?'

'Sure thing,' he agreed promptly. 'But what bothers me is: what about poor Arona? She's a total stranger to this Age and certainly not cut out for pioneering. I should say,' he added, studying her slender form, which looked rather odd in Len's borrowed jacket, 'that you are a hothouse plant, Arona.'

She smiled a little and gave Len a knowing glance.

'Anything but,' he said, standing up and looking about him. 'Her one love in life is activity and thrills, and in the rebuilding of a country — even of an entire civilisation — she will certainly get them.'

'Something,' Ena said slowly, 'is just beginning to register, Nick! I believe these two have fallen for each other!'

Len gave an embarrassed grin and Arona turned her head away — and in doing so she caught sight of something that made her gaze jerk upwards quickly. Something was speeding overhead, circling, an object like a cylinder.

'A time machine!' she gasped, pointing. 'Look!'

At the discovery she seemed to forget everything else She leapt to her feet and, seizing one of the biggest faggots from the fire began waving it wildly over her head. The men and women around her watched in wonder, entirely unaware that she was not a being of their own Age.

It seemed that at last those within the cylinder had seen her signals for the queer-shaped machine hovered directly overhead and then began to descend slowly, landing finally on the outer perimeter of the gathered people. Immediately there was a rush towards it, but Len, Arona, Nick and Ena got there first. They stood watching intently as the airlock opened.

A regal-looking individual appeared — grey haired, majestic, with a square-cut, determined face. His gaze went quickly over the throngs.

'Father!' Arona cried thankfully, hurling herself forward until she had seized him about the waist. 'Oh, thank heaven you found me!'

'It is indeed a relief to me, daughter,' her father replied gravely. 'When all the termites had gone and I found our race had freedom I had liberty to search for you. Since I could not find you I assumed you had somehow been caught up in the exodus to this age. The time-destination of the exodus had been registered on instruments, so I came back and searched. Fortunate that we saw your signals. We emerged by yonder big shaft — '

'Yes, yes, you would be bound to, that being the approximate same spot in our own Age,' Arona said. 'And — and I thought I was stranded here . . . '

Arona stopped. She had caught a glimpse of Len's face. It was filled with a bitter disappointment. The ruler of humanity in the year 6890 did not appear to notice his daughter's abrupt cessation of speech. He surveyed the gathered people calmly.

'My friends,' he said, 'I do not expect you to believe me when I tell you that I come from 6890. nearly five thousand years ahead of you, and this young woman here is my daughter. I think you should know that the termites you have defeated also came from a future Time, brought hither by discovering that some of their own giant breed had already been created by a misguided scientist. However, records of past time which I have found — future time to you, of course — state that such an ant invasion did take place in this year and that it was soundly beaten. Rest assured that in five more years, so our records show, your civilisation will be back to its former majesty, unimpaired.'

The survivors looked at one another, baffled.

'Time is a strange thing,' the ruler mused. 'In some cases it can give alternative directions — such as a civilisation where no ant menace has been heard of. In other cases it is an absolute straight line, as in this instance. The termites came to an age before their birth, true — just as I have done, and my daughter, but had the ants stayed any length of Time in this Age they would have found, themselves dissolving into nothing. The energy keeping them alive and evolved in 6890 would very gradually dissipate and leave them as nonentities. You cannot exist for long in a previous Time because it defeats Time law. As the discoverer of that law I know whereof I speak.'

'A moment, sir,' Len put in. 'Does that mean that if you, or Arona, stopped here for say, a year, you might disappear?'

'We would, my son,' the ruler assented impartially. 'And much sooner than a year, too. Six months would be the limit.'

'But Arona told me there were different states of Time and that — '

'Arona is still a child and young in such matters.' The ruler smiled indulgently as he looked at her. 'I, son, am a scientist. I was secretly pleased when the termites decided to go back into Time to conquer. I knew that they would destroy themselves by doing that — that is, had not other events taken a hand and destroyed them in a different way . . . '

'I've just thought of something,' Len said, frowning. 'The queen ant told us that their original invading force to our Time had started from 6960, nearly a hundred years ahead of yours and Arona's Time — that being the year they had conquered humanity.'

'That is correct. After their discovery of their origins, they augmented their forces here by recruiting ants from 6890, that being the time when they had all their weapons and military might already assembled. In 6960 they were so firmly in control they did not have the same military capability. But what is the point that puzzles you?'

'It's this, sir: if all of the ants in your age of 6890 have evacuated back here and been destroyed, how was it possible for them to be still ruling humanity in 6960? Surely they wouldn't have existed after your Time?'

'A paradox that is explicable from what I have already told you — there are several states of Time, and several alternate realities ... Do not worry yourself over the mysteries of Time, my son. Accept the reality of this moment and enjoy your life free of the ant menace.' The ruler paused, and looked at Arona.

'My mission here is finished now that I have found my daughter. It only remains for me to state my admiration for your courage and ingenuity. I have nothing more 1 can usefully add.'

'But — but, father — ' Arona hesitated, looking at her parent's stern yet somehow kindly face.

'Well, my child?'

'I — I think you should know. Before you appeared I had fully intended staying here. In fact I had no — choice.'

'You would have faded away, daughter. Becoming an abstract, meaningless nothing.'

'Which would have been a mighty shock for me!' Len exclaimed. 'Fancy a wife disappearing like mist!'

'A — wife?' the ruler asked deliberately, his brows down.

'Len — ' Arona nodded to him. 'Len and I had planned to marry. We're in love with each other.'

'I am not unwilling that the match should take place,' the ruler commented, studying Len intently. 'This young man appears strongly built and intelligent and obviously he must have won your heart . . . But it can never be, daughter, for the very reason that I have explained. You cannot stay here and continue to exist.'

Silence. Len looked about him desperately as the ruler's strong arm forced Arona gently towards the airlock.

'Sir — tell me, what would happen if *I* went into the future and tried to live there? Would that make me — evaporate?'

'No, my son.' There seemed to be a humorous twinkle somewhere in the keen eyes. 'When you move to a future state you are in a period in which you have not lived before and therefore have absolute freedom to develop.'

'That settles it!' Len declared, his eyes gleaming. 'I want permission, sir, to come to 6890 with you. I know it is an Age of tremendous power, especially now the termites have been wiped out, but even if it were not, even if it were in ruins, I'd come anyway — just to be with Arona.'

'You really mean this?' Nick asked blankly, catching Len's arm.

'Certainly I do. There'll be only pioneering and digging in this Age for a long time to come — and I'm nobody important, anyway, Nor have I anybody to leave behind. Different with you. You have Ena, and your lives to re-plan.'

'You are willing,' the ruler asked slowly, 'to plunge into a future Age, of which you know virtually nothing, just so that you may retain my daughter and make her your wife?'

'More than!'

The ruler smiled. 'I welcome such as you, my son. We too, have our rebuilding to do after the domination of the termites. Young men of virility are scarce in our age; the termites took them nearly all. Come . . . '

He stood aside, the eager girl beside him. Len hesitated for just a brief moment and then shook hands firmly with Ena and Nick. They were half smiling, but Ena was half crying.

'You've been such a friend, Len,' she

said. 'I can't bear the idea of losing you forever . . . '

' 'It is a far better thing' . . . ' he quoted, then to avoid further embarrassment he strode into the open airlock. The girl and the ruler followed him and the airlock closed. The machine did not rise into the air. Instead it became slowly transparent and finally vanished into the matrix of future years.

Nick drew a deep breath and put an arm about Ena's shoulders.

'That's that,' he murmured. 'Time you and I got on the move, old girl. We have an awful lot to do . . . '

## THE END

We do hope that you have enjoyed reading this large print book.

Did you know that all of our titles are available for purchase?

We publish a wide range of high quality large print books including:
**Romances, Mysteries, Classics**
**General Fiction**
**Non Fiction and Westerns**

Special interest titles available in large print are:
**The Little Oxford Dictionary**
**Music Book, Song Book**
**Hymn Book, Service Book**

Also available from us courtesy of Oxford University Press:
**Young Readers' Dictionary**
**(large print edition)**
**Young Readers' Thesaurus**
**(large print edition)**

For further information or a free brochure, please contact us at:
**Ulverscroft Large Print Books Ltd.,**
**The Green, Bradgate Road, Anstey,**
**Leicester, LE7 7FU, England.**
**Tel:** (00 44) **0116 236 4325**
**Fax:** (00 44) **0116 234 0205**

## MYSTERY OF THE CRATER

### John Glasby

Brander, the security chief of the Syrtis Base on Mars, isolates the entire emplacement when two men die from an unknown, alien disease. No one can enter or leave the base. Dr. John Naysmith, newly arrived on Mars, leads the medical team desperately trying discover a serum to combat the virus. If they can't contain the spread of the disease Brander must annihilate the base and everyone in it with nuclear bombs! Then another three men became infected . . .

# DR. MORELLE'S CASEBOOK

## Ernest Dudley

After a spate of time-wasting telephone calls, the Doctor had told Miss Frayle not to bother him with them; she must dismiss the callers and leave him to work on his thesis. But when the telephone rang again it was Professor Howard, clearly in the midst of a desperate struggle, wanting to speak to the Doctor on a matter of life and death. The Professor was being attacked — by spiders. So begins one of Doctor Morelle's strangest cases . . .